THE LONG SECRET

OTHER YEARLING BOOKS YOU WILL ENJOY:

HARRIET THE SPY, *Louise Fitzhugh*
SPORT, *Louise Fitzhugh*
ARE YOU THERE GOD? IT'S ME, MARGARET., *Judy Blume*
THEN AGAIN, MAYBE I WON'T, *Judy Blume*
BLUBBER, *Judy Blume*
IGGIE'S HOUSE, *Judy Blume*
OTHERWISE KNOWN AS SHEILA THE GREAT, *Judy Blume*
TALES OF A FOURTH GRADE NOTHING, *Judy Blume*
SUPERFUDGE, *Judy Blume*
FOURTH-GRADE CELEBRITY, *Patricia Reilly Giff*

YEARLING BOOKS are designed especially to entertain and enlighten young people. Charles F. Reasoner, Professor Emeritus of Children's Literature and Reading, New York University, is consultant to this series.

For a complete listing of all Yearling titles, write to Dell Publishing Co., Inc., Promotion Department, P.O. Box 3000, Pine Brook, N.J. 07058.

THE

LONG SECRET

Written and Illustrated by **LOUISE FITZHUGH**

A YEARLING BOOK

Published by
Dell Publishing Co., Inc.
1 Dag Hammarskjold Plaza
New York, New York 10017

Yearling ® TM 913705, Dell Publishing Co., Inc.

ISBN: 0-440-44977-4

Reprinted by arrangement with Harper & Row, Publishers, Inc.

Printed in the United States of America

One Previous Yearling Edition
New Yearling Edition
First printing—September 1984

MPC

For Connie, Dr. Slaff, and Ursula,
the nicest fanatics I know

THE LONG SECRET

Little Man's
Church

The Preacher's
house

The Jenkins'
house

The Montauk Highway

Supermarket
Laundry
Office
Candy store
Garage

the
Sharks
Tooth Inn

Beth
Ellen's
house

The
Beach

Harriet's
house

Mecox Bay

The
Clambar

CHAPTER 1

The notes were appearing everywhere. Everyone was talking about it. The first time Harriet and Beth Ellen ever saw anyone get one was one day in July when they were in the supermarket in Water Mill. They were standing at the checkout counter waiting to pay for their cookies. The woman with mean eyes who always checked them out was getting ready to charge them, when she suddenly drew her hand back from the cash register as though bitten by a snake.

"What in the world . . .?" she shrieked, and Harriet almost broke her stomach in two leaning over the counter to see. The woman held up a large piece of paper on which was written awkwardly in red crayon:

JESUS HATES YOU

"What is that? What in the world is that? Why would someone do that? What could they mean by that? Why would they say that to me? To me . . . to me?" The woman screamed on and on. A clerk came running. The manager of the store came running. Harriet stood with half-closed eyes, watching. Beth Ellen stared. Everyone began talking at once.

"Jake at the feed store got one."

"They're all over town. Everybody in Water Mill has gotten one."

"Why doesn't somebody do something? What is this?"

"They have. Mr. Jackson went to the police."

"What happened?"

"Well, they're looking around. What can they do? They can't find out who's doing it."

"Maybe they're protecting somebody."

"Yeah. Didn't have none of this all winter. One of those summer people flipped, maybe."

For some reason everyone turned and looked at Harriet and Beth Ellen. Harriet was so busy writing down everything in the notebook she always carried that she didn't notice, but Beth Ellen started to back out of the door.

"This all you have, kids?" The woman at the register suddenly became very sharp and businesslike.

"Yes," said Harriet in what she hoped was a disinterested way.

Beth Ellen was already out on the street. Harriet saw her streaking for the long, black car.

"Well, I'll tell you," said the checkout lady as she put the cookies in a bag, "there's some mighty strange people in these parts of a summer."

Harriet stood a minute with the bag in her hand, hoping the woman would say more, but she just looked at Harriet expectantly. Feeling foolish, Harriet turned abruptly and left the store.

Outside, she walked slowly to the car. The air on this early morning was sweet, faintly wet, and clinging. She felt the same nostalgic joy that she felt every year. The memories of every summer of her life seemed to make the air thick and rich. It was all so beautifully familiar: the short stretch of stores along the Montauk Highway, the flag in front of the tiny post office, the sign saying YOU ARE ENTERING WATER MILL, NEW YORK. SLOW DOWN AND ENJOY IT, which now was a virgin-white with black letters but by the end of the summer would be scrawled with drunken wit.

3

Even Beth Ellen, who sat waiting in the back seat of the big car driven by Harry, the Hansens' chauffeur, seemed a patient memory. Funny about Beth Ellen, thought Harriet as she climbed into the back seat, I never see her in the winter the way I do Janie and Sport, even though I go to school with her; and in the summer she's my best friend, just because she lives in Water Mill too, I guess.

The car glided off. She punched the button which raised the glass between the back seat and the front. She liked privacy. Besides, she liked pushing all those buttons.

"No, no," said Beth Ellen and pushed it again so that it lowered, "we have to tell him where we're going."

"I have to go to your house. I left my bike there," Harriet said, pushing the button again briskly. "Then shall we go to the beach?"

Beth Ellen looked frightened, but that was so much her normal expression that Harriet thought nothing of it. "I don't know if I can ride good enough to go that far."

"Sure you can. How're you ever going to learn if you don't try it? What good is a bike if you just ride around your driveway?"

"But I only learned a month ago." Beth Ellen began to munch a cookie in a distracted way.

"Well, I don't care if you come or not." Harriet

4

delivered this last looking sideways at Beth Ellen. It worked.

"I didn't say I wasn't going. I want to go."

"I know what let's do." Harriet made her eyes into slits and pushed them so far sideways her head hurt. "Let's just run past the Evil Hotel on the way."

Beth Ellen turned an intense red.

"Hee, hee," said Harriet and looked out the window.

"If you want to," said Beth Ellen, trying to look bored. She succeeded only in looking faintly sick to her stomach.

"If *I* want to!" said Harriet rudely. "HAH!"

"I thought you were writing a story about it," said Beth Ellen.

"I *am*," said Harriet, "but only because we've spent practically the whole summer there! I haven't anything else to write a story *about!* What have I seen this summer? Only that silly *Bunny!* And what have I *heard* this summer? Only that silly Bunny play the piano!" She sounded quite angry. "Well!" she said emphatically and stopped.

"Well, you don't have to come," said Beth Ellen with a little smile.

"I'm *coming*," said Harriet. "I have to finish my story now, don't I?" She grabbed for the cookie box and stuffed three in her mouth. Beth Ellen smiled. Harriet saw her and said with her mouth full, "Listen,

Mouse, for a mouse you sure get your own way all the time." Beth Ellen looked out the window to hide her tiny smile.

The car turned into the driveway of Beth Ellen's house. "I have to go and see my grandmother before I go," said Beth Ellen in a rather mournful way.

"That's okay," said Harriet. "I'll just fool around here." She didn't even look at Beth Ellen, because she was watching Harry. She had been spying on him all summer, and he bore careful watching. Harry seemed to lead a very curious life.

"And anyway," said Beth Ellen as she slammed the door to the car, "it's you that call it the Evil Hotel. I don't."

Harriet started to shout something after her, but Beth Ellen shot through the door. *Hhrumph*, she thought, I just called it that to bug her. I never saw anybody with such a crush. I hope I never have one.

She marched off to the servants' quarters, which were attached to the garage. Covering her course as well as she could by a row of hedges, she stationed herself at the window of Harry's room.

CHAPTER 2

Beth Ellen knocked on her grandmother's door.
"Come in," came a sharp voice from behind the door.
She walked in and saw her grandmother propped
against a mass of pillows. Susie, the maid, was standing beside the bed, looking very pale.

"Hello, darling. Come in and sit down," said her
grandmother, giving her a brief smile and turning
back to the maid. Beth Ellen went over and sat on
the chaise.

"It is not a question of that," her grandmother continued to Susie. "I do not want to go into it any further. I simply want it understood that it is not to
happen again."

Beth Ellen looked up at the strange sound in her grandmother's voice. Mrs. Hansen's voice was an unusually soft one most of the time, but today it sounded brittle, clipped, hard. Her face seemed cold. Susie looked frightened.

"That's all now," said Mrs. Hansen and turned to Beth Ellen as Susie left the room. "Well, dear, are you off to the beach?"

"Yes," said Beth Ellen simply and looked at the floor. She never knew quite what to talk about with her grandmother. She always wanted to sparkle and say a lot of things that would interest her, make her look up and gasp at Beth Ellen's wit and sophistication. But she was always overcome by shyness, by a timidity so powerful it turned her mind to dough.

Looking up from the floor, Beth Ellen realized that her grandmother was not thinking about her at all, was in fact looking out of the window with a rather angry expression. When she began to speak, she continued to look out the window.

"The importance of remaining a lady at all times cannot be overestimated. There are moments when this becomes very trying."

Beth Ellen had heard this speech a number of times. She knew what it meant. It meant "Don't get angry." There were other versions such as "Ladies never lose control," "Composure is the first mark of breeding," and "There is no sight so ugly as the hu-

8

man face in anger," but they all meant the same thing.

Mrs. Hansen continued: "Susie has given me cause at this very moment to become enraged. . . . A very simple thing she did, really. . . . I suppose an old woman gets crotchety . . . but she MOVED my perfume bottles!"

Beth Ellen felt like laughing but restrained herself.

"We must always leave it to God to carry out our punishments." Mrs. Hansen had turned to face Beth Ellen as she said this and now seemed to see her for the first time. She smiled as though she weren't mad at all and said in a sweet voice, "I meant to tell you, darling, I think you'll have a lovely surprise in a few weeks!"

"Oh, what?" asked Beth Ellen, wondering if they were to take a trip.

"I don't want to tell you now because it may not happen, but this time I am fairly sure it will."

Beth Ellen looked at her expectantly. "What is it?"

"Oh, but it wouldn't be a surprise then, would it, dear?" Mrs. Hansen had a beautiful smile when she really smiled. "You'd better run along, hadn't you, darling? You don't want to miss all that lovely sunshine."

Beth Ellen got up and went to receive a kiss on her forehead.

"Have a good time, dear," her grandmother said absently as Beth Ellen closed the door.

9

CHAPTER 3

When she got downstairs, Beth Ellen found Harriet laughing her head off.

"What's funny?" asked Beth Ellen, beginning clumsily to climb onto her bicycle.

"Harry got one of those notes, and I stole it after he left his room, as evidence," Harriet said triumphantly.

"Evidence?"

"Sure, we're going to catch this note leaver." Harriet was straddling her bike, looking at the note with a magnifying glass. Naturally she just saw some big

10

red letters. "Here, look at this." She passed the note to Beth Ellen, who read:

NO MAN CAN SERVE TWO MASTERS

"What's funny about that?" Beth Ellen asked.

"Don't you know?"

Beth Ellen shook her head.

"Well," said Harriet, looking pompous, "I happen to know something you don't know, then, and that is that Harry has been running a limousine service with that car. When he's supposed to be sitting here waiting to see if your grandmother wants to go anywhere, he's out taking people to the airport and all over town, even New York."

"Really?" said Beth Ellen in a bored way. "I wondered where he went all the time."

"You're a rotten spy, Beth Ellen." Harriet said this in such a matter-of-fact way that it didn't even bother Beth Ellen, who didn't want to be a spy anyway, rotten or otherwise. "What I don't get is how the person who wrote this knew that." Harriet didn't even look to Beth Ellen for an answer but just pushed off on her bike. Beth Ellen took off after her, wobbling a bit but upright.

Harriet zoomed out of the driveway with Beth Ellen careening after her. When they got to the end, there was a small hill and Beth Ellen fell off.

11

"Did you hurt yourself?" Harriet asked, having wheeled expertly around and gone back to where Beth Ellen lay flat, a startled expression on her face.

"No, I don't think so." She picked herself up as though she were glass, looked herself all over, then stubbornly picked up the bike.

"Listen"—Harriet was making a quick spot check of the tools hanging from the belt hooks in her shorts, so she didn't look up—"I think we'll go first to look at that new family." Everything was there: her flashlight, boy scout knife, canteen, pouch for pencils, and pouch for notebooks. She was carrying two notebooks this year, the one regularly used for spying and a new one for writing.

"I thought we were going to the hotel," Beth Ellen said ever so casually. She was picking a scab on her knee.

"Keep cool," said Harriet. "We'll get there. After." She pushed off on her bike. "First let's go see the family. This is Friday, you know," she said over her shoulder.

"So what?" yelled Beth Ellen. Beth Ellen was given to sudden yells.

Harriet called back over her shoulder, "That Mama Jenkins they keep talking about arrives from the city today for the weekend. I want to see what she looks like."

Beth Ellen was too engrossed in the hazards of the

12

road to answer, so they went on a way in silence. The road led down a hill, past potato fields, along a low flat place with three trees in the distance. In about three minutes they reached the Montauk Highway. Harriet stopped short and Beth Ellen skidded up behind her.

"Be careful. Now we go across there and up that little road by the filling station." Harriet looked up and down and then pushed off there being not a car in sight.

Beth Ellen followed, and they rode along through the summer day. The sun lay flat and heavy on the potato fields. The handlebars were hot to the touch. After a long road, a turn, and another long road, Harriet pulled up under a shade tree. It was cool, and their eyes began to see everything as very green.

"It's right over there—the second little house—but we're getting too close now, we might be seen. So I think we better leave our bikes here and sneak around the back." Harriet was very efficient. Beth Ellen's heart began to rattle a little.

Harriet propped her bike against the tree on one side, and Beth Ellen started to put hers there, then remembered the support stick and took a little time getting it to come down.

"Come on," said Harriet, not a little irritated.

They were finally ready and started to sneak around the house. As they were coming around a hedge in the back a very fat boy of about their age came waddling across one of the back fields.

"That's Norman," whispered Harriet, "the boy twin. He's a pill."

"How old are they?" asked Beth Ellen.

"They're twelve," said Harriet. "Wait'll you see the other one."

Beth Ellen looked at Norman. He was rather like a gingerbread man. He had a round blob of a body with a round freckled face stuck on top, round arms, and useless splayed-out-looking legs which looked trapped in his bathing trunks. He wore enormous black high sneakers, heavy white socks, and a dirty-looking T-shirt. He went into the second house in the row.

They started sneaking again and this time got past the first house. As they approached the side window that Harriet used she turned suddenly and whispered, "Remember the rules: not a sound. And if anything happens, we were just walking through this yard because we lost a ball here."

Beth Ellen nodded, petrified.

They crept to the window and looked in. There was a large sunny kitchen with three children in it. One of them was Norman. There was also a thin girl of the same height, with long, straight brown hair. There was a tiny girl of about four, who sat at the table.

"I want a quarter," growled Norman in the direction of his twin. He had a voice like a gravel pit.

14

"Why, Norman Jenkins, you just don't get no quarter," said the twin, all sweetness and light.

"I want my quarter."

"Quawter, quawter, quawter," crooned the four-year-old.

"I gets a quarter when I wants a quarter. Mama Jenkins said so." Norman began to shout.

"Now you just hush your mouth, Norman Jenkins. You gets a quarter when you're *good,* and I haven't seen anything very *good.* 'The *Lord* will provide.' That's what Mama Jenkins said. You didn't listen real good. The *Lord* will *provide* when you're *good.*"

"I'm GOOD." Norman looked like he might sock her.

"Why, you . . . you just tell me one little old good thing you did this week!"

They looked at each other in a stalemate. Norman couldn't think of a thing.

"Jessie Mae?" piped the four-year-old.

"Yes, Magnolia, what?"

Jessie Mae! thought Harriet.

"When duth Mama Jenkinth come?" Magnolia wasn't easy to understand, particularly with her mouth full.

"She gets here tonight at seven, honey, the Lord willing," Jessie Mae said and turned her back.

"You're supposed to give me my allowance." Norman kept at it. "Matter of fact, I don't know why you

15

have charge of it. Why can't I give you your allowance just as well?"

"You *know* why—Mama Jenkins told you—because you care too much about money and I walk with God."

"You don't walk with God a damned bit more than I do!" Norman yelled this, he was so mad.

"That just goes to show you. Cursing. We don't have a lot of money to waste on people who are bad." Jessie Mae didn't even look at him.

"We're RICH now." He stood in the middle of the room and bellowed. His fat face turned orange.

"Why are we rich?" asked Magnolia.

"Because, little darling"—Jessie Mae had a sing-song way of talking—"Mama has invented something."

"What?"

Magnolia and Jessie Mae went on talking as though Norman weren't standing there fuming.

"Something for toes. A toe medicine."

"What she make it out of?" Magnolia looked up with real interest.

"Chicken do!" screamed Norman and went off into an avalanche of gravelly laughter.

"Listen here, Norman Jenkins, you gonna get it right across the mouth," yelled Jessie Mae, losing her temper altogether.

"I don't care, you old bag," Norman threw over his

shoulder as he scurried for safety into the living room.

"Chicken do, chicken do, chicken do," sang Magnolia.

"Magnolia, you hush up. It is not. It's made out of watermelons, in fact. Watermelons and several secret ingredients that no one knows but Mama Jenkins." Jessie Mae looked terribly affronted.

Magnolia said abruptly, "I want another pickle sandwich."

"You've had two; that's enough," said Jessie Mae calmly, turning back to the dishes.

"Pickles and wettice. Pickles and wettice." Magnolia beat on the table with one small fist.

"There's no more lettuce. Go out and play now, darling," Jessie Mae said quietly.

Harriet wrote in her notebook:

WHO EVER HEARD OF A PICKLE AND LETTUCE SANDWICH? NOW FOR MY MONEY THERE IS NOTHING IN THE WORLD LIKE A TOMATO SANDWICH.

Beth Ellen whispered, "I'm hungry." And just as Harriet was putting her finger to her lips to shush her they heard an awful grinding of gears and the racing of a motor. There was no time to run, because right into the very driveway where they were standing plummeted a white Maseratti. It scorched to a stop about one foot from where they stood and enveloped

17

them immediately in a cloud of dust.

The door slammed and an enormous woman leapt from the driver's seat like a kangaroo and hopped right over to them through the dust before they could even move.

"Why, looky here what's in my driveway," she shouted cheerfully and slammed one fat hand down on each of their heads. They were immobilized and rolled their eyes up to see her round, laughing face. Her hands and arms were red, her face and neck a mass covered with freckles and sweat.

Harriet looked her over carefully. She wore what might be called the most basic black dress in the world. It hugged her expressively, then hung in rivulets around the hem. The short sleeves were oddly gathered and hung in folds over the huge hamlike rolls of her freckled arms. She didn't have the ordinary amount of teeth, and Harriet stared, fascinated, at the ones she did have.

The mountain shivered and shook, and there issued forth a great cackle like spring thunder. "Ask and the Lord will provide. You little chickens want to work for me?"

Jessie Mae slammed out of the back door, with Magnolia right behind her, and Norman came charging around from the front.

"Mama Jenkins, Mama Jenkins, Mama Jenkins!" they all screamed with one voice.

"Hi, younguns, looky what I found looking in the window!" Mama Jenkins turned her hands, thereby swiveling the necks of her prizes. She had a voice like a foghorn. "These here friends of yours?"

The three children stopped, silent and staring. They looked Harriet and Beth Ellen over inch by inch.

"They're *girls,*" said Norman with disgust, indicating clearly that they couldn't be friends of his.

"Dirls, dirls, dirls," said Magnolia, laughing and jumping up and down.

"I have never had the pleasure," said Jessie Mae primly.

What old trunk did she get that out of, thought Harriet.

"Well," droned Mama Jenkins with what seemed a great deal of joy, "what you think I should do with them?"

"Make them work," croaked Norman.

"What was they doing here?" asked Jessie Mae.

"Let's eat 'em," howled Magnolia, falling on the ground with her own humor.

"They appeared to be looking into our kitchen," said Mama Jenkins.

"They look like they want to go home," said Jessie Mae.

"Yep," said Mama Jenkins regretfully, "reckon you're right. Too bad we can't keep them, though.

Mighty cute. Oughta be good for something." And so saying she gave them each a playful shove with her great paws.

She laughed loudly. She kept looking at them for a minute, then she leaned over so close to their faces that they could smell her breath, which smelled, curiously enough, of watermelon pickle. She stood like this for what seemed a long time and then said "SCAT!" so suddenly and so loudly that they both fled down the drive.

They ran so fast and in such a jumble that they tripped over each other and both went sprawling.

They sat there in the dirt, looking back at the house. Mama Jenkins laughed again, then started back toward the house. "She walks like a truck," said Harriet under her breath.

The kids followed their mother, clamoring around her heels like a litter of puppies. Jessie Mae did look back once, curiously, as one might at a dead snake in the road.

When they had disappeared into the house, Harriet got up, picked up her notebook, and brushed herself off. Beth Ellen was slower.

"Come on," said Harriet, "let's get out of here." She looked down at Beth Ellen, who looked stunned. It was the first time she had ever seen Beth Ellen look dirty. There were smudges of dirt on her face. For a moment she felt sorry for her.

"Well, I never told you it was easy," she said briskly. She put out a hand to help her up. Beth Ellen didn't say anything, but Harriet knew she was wondering why she had come. "Maybe we should go to the beach," Harriet said quickly.

"No," said Beth Ellen in a faint but plucky voice, "the hotel."

As they sneaked past the window they heard voices and stopped to listen. "What you want that quarter for, boy?" Mama Jenkins stood over Norman like Moses at the burning bush.

Norman rolled his eyes, hesitated, then said, "There's a tabernacle meeting down to Bridgehampton." He rolled his eyes as if they were marbles.

"Why, Norman Jenkins, there's no such thing. You want that quarter for ice cream. Mama, he eats three quarts of ice cream a *day!*" Jessie Mae was the picture of outrage.

"What's wrong with that?" asked Mama Jenkins.

"MAMA, it's *gluttony!*" screeched Jessie Mae.

"Well, now," said Mama Jenkins, repressing a smile, "is there a meeting or is there not a meeting?"

Norman rolled his eyes. "There was a poster which said there *might* be a meeting."

"So, just in case, you want a quarter. Right? Just in case next year they has a meeting?" Mama Jenkins looked arch. Jessie Mae let out a shrill, affected laugh. Norman kicked her in the shin.

22

Mama Jenkins leaned over and grabbed Norman's shirt front. "Listen here, boy, what you want that quarter for?"

"For ice cream!" screamed Norman, purple and wiggling.

"I reckon, Norman dear, that you gonna start your diet on Monday, ain't that right?" asked Jessie Mae sweetly.

"Diet?" Mama Jenkins turned a horrified face to Jessie Mae. "What's the matter with the way he looks?"

Harriet threw up her hands at this idiocy, and they walked over to their bikes.

CHAPTER 4

When they got to their bikes, the sun was so hot that they rode slowly.

"Harriet?"

"Yes?"

"Why are you doing all this spying around?"

"Because"—Harriet was so exasperated she began to shout—"I'm going to be a writer and I have to have something to write, don't I? I'm not like you, going and looking at people just because I think they're nice. And besides, you know what? I'm going to catch that note leaver!" She got such a spurt of energy from her own enthusiasm that she shot ahead on her bike.

Oh, Harriet, thought Beth Ellen, you are always Harriet. She pumped on doggedly, trying to keep up.

"And besides," said Harriet, falling back a little bit, "I thought you were going to be a writer too. Last year when we both worked on the paper at school, I thought you liked it."

"I don't think I like it," said Beth Ellen, looking uncomfortable as though writing were an itchy sweater.

"Why don't you write about this Bunny you're so hooked on? *I'm* writing about Bunny, and *you* should be the one writing about Bunny. I'm not even in love with him!"

"I don't want to write about him, I want to marry him," said Beth Ellen.

"Well!" said Harriet, "that's the most ridiculous thing I ever heard. You're only eleven."

"Twelve."

"How can you be twelve when I'm only eleven?" Harriet looked furious.

Beth Ellen waited.

"Oh, that's right," said Harriet finally. "I always forget that about birthdays. I remember, you just had one."

"Yes," said Beth Ellen simply and fell into a reverie about her birthday party. A piano had been put outdoors and Bunny had played. Some terrible little boys were there that they were supposed to dance with, but Beth Ellen had spent the whole time at the piano. She had finally been dragged away by the maid, at her grandmother's orders, and forced to sit down and watch a magician with a shiny black suit and a red nose.

"*I* was born in *October*," said Harriet as though October were the only really satisfactory month to be born in. Beth Ellen looked at her blankly.

They crossed the highway and went on toward the hotel. It sat along a country road in Water Mill. They saw the sign which said SHARK'S TOOTH INN. There was a story going around that the inn had gotten its name when the original owner—a fat, chuckling sea captain—had been eaten by a shark.

The inn was very old and sat comfortably nestled in a little dell, surrounded by beautiful and ancient trees. The inn itself was a lovely, high-ceilinged, rambling structure which had been redecorated by its present owner, a fat, chuckling society woman.

Whenever Harriet and Beth Ellen saw the inn, it looked cool and quiet—its awnings protecting it against the sun—but the goings-on at night were rumored to be extraordinary. There was never anyone around in the daytime except the chef and his wife and, of course, Bunny. This made Beth Ellen intensely happy but frustrated Harriet because she had never even caught sight of the owner, who didn't appear until the dinner hour. Harriet had tried, unsuccessfully so far, to talk her parents into taking her to dinner there. They always responded with the same strange looks, and each time had dropped the subject immediately.

They propped their bikes against the hedge and were about to sneak around the back, because that was Bunny's favorite place for a sunbath, when they heard a shout. They ducked down and went around a garbage can, then behind another hedge. They lay on their stomachs, and once comfortably settled, they looked toward the back door.

At the back door was a screened porch which held an enormous walk-in refrigerator. Into this was walking a short, balding man with a long scar on his face. He opened the refrigerator door, walked in, walked out again immediately, then yelled through the screened door into the kitchen.

"*Bon, bon, bon, bon, BON! Tu vois! Il n'y a rien dans ce frigidaire!*"

A round little woman with a frightened face came bustling through the kitchen door. She peered into the icebox.

"*Qu'est-ce que tu racontes?*" he bellowed at her.

"*Mais, voilà la note!*" She pointed with one wavering finger.

Beth Ellen was trying desperately to remember any of the French taught to her by Mademoiselle Shwartz

27

at The Gregory School, but all she could think of was *crayon*. She looked over at Harriet, who appeared to be understanding every word and was just patiently listening.

"*Mais où?*" The man stuck his bull neck into the icebox.

"*Là, là, sur la viande.*"

At least I understand that, thought Beth Ellen.

The man reached in with one beefy hand and drew out a small piece of paper. He looked at it, then at his wife. "*Mais, c'est quoi, ça?*"

"*C'est ça. C'est ce que je t'ai dis, ce matin,*" she replied.

Furious, he turned on her. "*Tu dois la lire. Tu sais bien que je ne peux pas lire l'anglais.*"

The woman began painfully to try to read in English. "A saft . . . ansuer . . . toornet aweigh . . . rat." She shrugged.

He shrugged. "*Ça veut dire quoi?*" he asked, looking even more angry than before.

"*Sais pas.*" She shrugged again.

Harriet whispered, "What are they saying?" and Beth Ellen shrugged. It was catching.

There was a sudden hoarse yell from the direction of the cottages behind the hotel.

"Moo-Moo, Moooooo, come here this minute!" The voice sounded not only hoarse but rather strangled. "Help, somebody, there she goes again!"

28

"That was Bunny!" said Beth Ellen wildly.

Harriet was so curious she almost ran out from behind the hedge and had to be restrained by Beth Ellen.

The couple on the porch became very agitated. The man threw his hands up and said, *"Ooo, là, c'est Moo-Moo encore!"* Both of them flew off the porch and around the hotel toward the voice.

There was much screaming and carrying on for a few minutes, and then suddenly around the hedge lunged an apparition. It was very fat, with extremely short little legs, and had large brown and white spots all over it. It looked, in fact, like a small cow.

It tore around the hedge and Harriet lay rooted to the spot, knowing full well the pursuers would be right behind. Moo-Moo careened right past them and onto the back porch, there to sit expectantly, almost laughing.

Around the hedge came Bunny. Harriet drew back, not so much not to be seen as not to be hit by a flying espadrille. Bunny wore a tiny bikini, an immense shirt which hid his somewhat rotund body, and a large, floppy straw hat. Beth Ellen gasped.

Trundling behind Bunny came first the scarred chef, then his dumpy wife, who waddled and panted trying to keep up.

"There you are, my Moo, my nuddle Moo-Moo,"

cooed Bunny, picking up the small cow and cradling
it in his arms.

"*Eh, voilà,*" said the chef. His wife just panted.
They all looked at the dog. "He try always to run
away," said the chef cleverly.

"You'd think you didn't like it here, Moo-Moo,"
said Bunny, looking down soulfully into the dog's
eyes. Moo-Moo jumped out of his arms, went to a
bowl, and drank some water.

He's bored, thought Harriet. That is one bored
dog.

"Hey, Bunny," said the chef, "we find somezing zis
morning in zee box."

"What?" asked Bunny, his eyes on Moo-Moo.

The chef handed him the note. He looked at it a
long time, then read aloud:

A SOFT ANSWER TURNETH AWAY WRATH

They all three looked at each other and then Bunny
burst out laughing. He laughed and laughed. He
laughed so hard that he had to bend over and clutch
his stomach.

The chef looked affronted. The chef's wife started
to giggle. She put her hand up to her face to hide her
giggles. The chef looked at her with rage. "*Eh, bien,
quoi?*" he said loudly, throwing his hands up in the
air.

30

"Apt, old boy," said Bunny, his laughter having subsided, "terribly, cruelly apt."

"Hapt?" said the chef in dismay.

"Well . . ." said Bunny.

The chef's wife giggled loudly. The chef turned as though to smack her, and Bunny interceded: "After all, you gave me such a tearing into last week, I thought I wouldn't even be able to play."

Harriet and Beth Ellen looked at each other and nodded. They had been there.

"Here, though," continued Bunny, taking a piece of paper from his voluminous shirt, "just to make you feel better, I got a whopper this morning." He looked around to check on Moo's whereabouts, then read aloud in a stentorian voice:

WOE UNTO THEM THAT RISE UP EARLY IN THE MORNING THAT THEY MAY FOLLOW STRONG DRINK

The chef started laughing very loudly and rather meanly. The wife joined in, and the three of them laughed together. Bunny had an infectious laugh that could be heard for a block.

"I don't think that's so funny," said Beth Ellen primly. "He really shouldn't drink so much."

"That's not why they're laughing, dopey," whispered Harriet. "They're laughing because whoever writes those things knows him so well."

"And yesterday," said Bunny, "I got this one!" He searched through his pockets again, and taking the paper out, read:

DESPISE NOT THY MOTHER WHEN SHE IS OLD

He looked down at the note for a long time, suddenly serious. "Which just *might* give us a clue as to who's leaving these little darlings around."

Harriet leaned forward eagerly. She turned and said *"Hmmmmm"* very loudly to Beth Ellen. Beth Ellen looked totally disinterested in the notes, only continuing to stare at Bunny with longing.

"Boy," said Harriet, "how love can poison the mind. Listen, I'm going to come around here even more. This is such a big place, they obviously get more notes; so that note leaver will have to be here more often, right?"

Beth Ellen nodded sappily, her eyes never leaving Bunny for a minute.

"Speak of the devil," said Bunny and looked down the driveway. Hobbling across, with a cane, was a wretched-looking little old lady. As she approached the back porch she began to whine, "Uh, I slept so badly. Oh, dear, another attack. Oh, me, oh, my, I feel awful."

"Oh, swell," said Bunny, slapping a hand against his leg, "another smashing start to another smashing

33

day, another riotous morning at the Shark's Tooth Inn!"

"Son, I just don't understand you, bringing me to a place like this. My arthritis is killing me, and this place is one of the dampest places in America."

Bunny fled indoors, his great shirt and Moo-Moo flapping behind him. The chef and his wife went through the door too as though they were all being herded in by the old lady's words. She grumbled her way in after them and slammed the screen door.

Harriet and Beth Ellen waited a minute but nothing more happened. Beth Ellen sighed. "Oh, for goodness' sake," said Harriet.

They crawled out from under the hedge. Their shirts were brown with mud. Harriet took out her notebook, which never left her side and in which she wrote down everything that happened to her. Beth Ellen put a finger in her mouth as though a tooth hurt.

Harriet wrote down everything, putting many exclamation points after some comments on Beth Ellen's attitude toward Bunny, then added this coda:

NOW THE THING IS WHO WOULD LEAVE NOTES LIKE THIS? SOMEBODY WHO READS THE BIBLE BECAUSE THEY ALL SOUND LIKE THEY'RE RIGHT OUT OF THE BIBLE. WHO DOES READ THE BIBLE? DOES ANYBODY? DOES MY MOTHER? FIND OUT. CHECK ON THIS.

CHAPTER 5

She put her book away and woke up Beth Ellen, who was standing in a trance. "You want to go to the beach?"

"*Yes,*" said Beth Ellen and smiled a really happy smile. They jumped on their bikes, and turning them around, headed for the beach.

Once there they put their bikes on the top of the hill where they could watch them from the beach. Harriet took her yellow beach towel, her lunch, and her notebooks out of the basket and started thumping down the hill. Beth Ellen had a drawing pad with her as well as her lunch and a bright orange and white beach towel.

The sand was hot. There was no wind. The sand burned their ankles and got into their sneakers. They trudged on toward the water, where it was cooler.

Harriet looked around for a good place. She found one not too far from two young mothers sitting guard on two toddlers and engaged in a spirited conversation. She hoped she would be able to overhear them without being too obvious.

They spread out their towels. Beth Ellen took off her shorts, sneakers, and shirt, and sat down in her bathing suit. She looked at the ocean and found it, after Bunny, dull.

Harriet took off her shirt, her shorts with the hooks and tools for spying, her sneakers, and ran like blazes toward the water. Her red and white striped suit made a pink streak, she went so fast. Beth Ellen stared, then jumped and followed. Harriet was leaping like a wild thing out to sea. When it covered her stomach, she dove under a wave. Beth Ellen watched her with envy. She could never, like Harriet, just run straight into the water. She always had to coax herself, sidle a little along the coast, then hold her nose and run at the moment she least expected it. Years of swimming instruction at various resorts had come to nothing because of her conviction that the minute she went in she would sink.

She rushed in, her heart thumping horribly. It

36

wasn't too cold. She got wet all over, then looked around for Harriet. Harriet seemed to be going to Europe. "Hey!" she yelled after the bobbing head.

Harriet stopped abruptly and stood up. The water was shallow. Beth Ellen felt rather an idiot to be so afraid in such shallow water.

"Hey, Mouse! Come on out here!" Harriet yelled. Beth Ellen plowed along through the knee-high water. Even so, when a wave hit her, she thought she was done for.

They played and swam for a long time, the hot sun burning their backs and faces, the cool water all around them a long blue going into nowhere.

"Let's eat," said Harriet, and they started back. Harriet found a small wave to ride a bit of the way in, but Beth Ellen kept up an unsteady walk, always looking back to see if a wave were going to drown her.

When they got back to the towels, all wet and hot again and tasting of salt, they plunked down and both grabbed for their lunch bags. Beth Ellen picked a sandwich out and started to eat it.

"What is that?" asked Harriet.

"Pimento cheese."

Harriet got out several sandwiches, all tomato. Beth Ellen knew they would all be tomato, so she didn't even ask. They were always tomato. For as long as Beth Ellen could remember, Harriet had brought tomato sandwiches to school in the winter and to the beach in the summer.

Through one of these Harriet asked, "Did you understand all that French?"

"Was it French?" answered Beth Ellen, looking out to sea and chewing. She was suddenly irritated with Harriet and her tomato sandwiches.

Harriet's eyes widened. "You know, sometimes, Beth Ellen, I wonder where you keep yourself."

Beth Ellen looked at her once but didn't show any emotion, nor did she seem to be thinking of anything. They continued to eat in silence.

Harriet strained her ears to hear what the two young mothers were saying to each other, but she could only hear the ocean. Maybe, she thought, if I put a shell to my ear I could hear their conversation. She laughed to herself but decided not to tell Beth Ellen because it sounded bats. Sometimes it was hard to talk to Beth Ellen because she would stare at you with such round, blank eyes that you would begin to wonder what you'd said.

Harriet got out her notebook and looked over her notes. "Who do you think could be doing this?" she asked Beth Ellen.

"What?" asked Beth Ellen.

"Leaving the *notes!*" screamed Harriet. Really, sometimes the girl seemed daft.

"Oh," said Beth Ellen, turning enormous eyes on Harriet, "I can't imagine."

"Hhrumph!" said Harriet with disapproval.

Beth Ellen continued to stare until Harriet looked back at her notebook. Then she picked up her drawing pad and a pencil. She started to draw a fat lady being eaten by a turtle, but she got bored with it and began to draw the two mothers and their children.

Harriet put down her notebook which contained her spy notes and picked up the one in which she was writing a story called "The Evil Hotel." She read over what she had written last and found it splendid.

She turned over a few pages because she didn't want to continue the story today. She had been trying for two days to write a poem.

She had recently discovered poetry and something about the economy of it appealed to her. She sat still, very still, looking at the water but thinking of a day last fall. On that day she had stood in the park across the street from her school in New York. She had watched the Good Humor man blow his nose in a bright blue handkerchief.

It had been about to rain and she felt lost. Feelings that just appeared and were not attached to anything had always fascinated her. She wrote:

IT WAS GOING TO RAIN

She looked at it, then crossed it out and wrote:

BEFORE THE RAIN

40

She then wrote:

THE PARK

And changed it to:

THE WORLD

Now she had:

BEFORE THE RAIN

THE WORLD

She sat thinking about how the park had looked that day, so green, so expectant, still, and tense. She thought of words like "waiting," "hushed," "tired," but it was not any of these. She thought of "young." She began to put things together like "waiting green," "hurting grass," "a frightened tree." Then, suddenly, she wrote down:

BEFORE THE RAIN

THE WORLD

IS GREEN

But the rest had to be there. She suddenly wanted it to rhyme. What rhymed with rain? Rain, cane, mane. She decided to go through the alphabet:

Ain (nothing).

Bain (nothing . . . oh, yes, Bane).

Cane.

Dane (a great Dane in the park?).

Hane (nothing).

Oh, dear, she thought, I forgot the alphabet.

Dane.

Eain (nothing).

Fain (feign?).

Gain (with nothing to gain?).

No. Thinking of the phrase again, she cringed a little and thought, Boring. This is a little like playing Scrabble, she thought happily and plunged in again.

Hane (nothing).

I (nothing).

Jane (Janie?).

Kane (nothing).

Lane (and in the park, a lane? Maybe. No. Stinks).

Mane.

Nane (nothing).

O (nothing).

Pain (oh, there!).

It *felt* like a pain, that look the world had. She wrote it down:

AND FILLED WITH PAIN

No. Not that. She changed it to:

AND FULL OF PAIN

Not that. That's worse. She crossed it out and wrote:

AND IN PAIN

She thought fleetingly of throwing out the whole thing. But, no, it was fun. She threw out the line instead.

Q (nothing).

Rain (already there).

Sain (sane? insane? Maybe. No).

Tane (nothing).

U (nothing).

Vain (is vain? AH! Well, perhaps).

X (nothing).

Y (nothing).

Z (nothing).

Hhrumph, she thought, and sat chewing the two thoughts, vain and pain. She looked around the beach. Nothing much had changed. Beth Ellen was lying on her stomach, drawing with her nose quite close to the paper.

"What are you drawing?" asked Harriet, twisting around to look at her.

"A house on fire," said Beth Ellen calmly.

"You like to draw, don't you?" asked Harriet.

"Yes."

"Then are you going to be an artist?"

"I don't know."

"Be an artist," said Harriet, dismissing Beth Ellen as a solved problem.

Beth Ellen sat up and looked at the back of Harriet's neck for a long time. "I don't," she said quietly, "want to be anything at all."

Harriet didn't turn around but said, "That's ridiculous. How can you do that?"

"I want to grow up and marry a rich man. I want to have a little boy and, maybe, a little girl. I want to go to Biarritz."

Harriet stared at her. "That's the most boring thing I ever heard of." She looked straight into Beth Ellen's eyes.

Beth Ellen looked back at her.

"Anyway, what's there?" asked Harriet.

"Where?" said Beth Ellen, knowing full well what she meant.

"BIARRITZ!" screamed Harriet. "BETH ELLEN, SOMETIMES YOU GET ON MY NERVES!"

"Well," said Beth Ellen, thinking: My mother is in Biarritz.

"Listen," said Harriet patiently as though to a little child, "you're only twelve. You'll get over this."

"I will not."

"You have to. What do you want to do? Sponge off somebody?"

"Yes."

"You'll be boring. You'll be a very boring person." Harriet was getting very red in the face. "No one will come and see you. *I* certainly won't come and see you. *I'll* be working. I won't have *time* for that nonsense. You'll be asking me to look at your babies' pictures. You'll ask everybody to look at these dumb snapshots all the time and nobody will want to look." Harriet stopped rather suddenly, having realized that she was screaming. What is the matter with me? she thought; I don't care what she does.

44

"I'm going to have lots of babies and go to Biarritz," said Beth Ellen with authority and rolled over on her stomach again.

There was silence. Well, thought Harriet. She picked up the notebook in which she made notes on people and wrote:

YOU JUST NEVER KNOW ABOUT PEOPLE. WHY WOULD ANYONE WANT TO DO THAT? SHE'S FLIPPED HER WIG. MAYBE I SHOULD CONSIDER HAVING BABIES. DO I WANT A BABY? WHAT WOULD I DO WITH IT? IT WOULD ALL THE TIME BE CRYING AND WANTING TO BE FED. AND ALL THOSE DIAPERS. WELL.

She put down both books and lay on her back. She tried to stare right into the sun. She couldn't.

CHAPTER 6

Three days later Beth Ellen was sitting in her room, writing herself a letter.

> *Dear Me,*
> *Why am I so different? Why am I never happy? Is everybody like this or is it just me? I am truly a mouse. I have no desire at all to be me.*
>
> > *Good-bye,*
> > *Mouse*

The telephone rang. Beth Ellen heard the maid answer downstairs, then call to her, "Miss Beth! Miss Beth, for you." She got up and went into her grandfa-

ther's room to answer because there wasn't a phone in her room.

"Hello?"

"Hi." It was Harriet.

"Why don't you come over?" Beth Ellen asked, feeling suddenly lonely.

"It's *raining*," said Harriet with great irritation. "You come over here because Harry can bring you and I've only got the bicycle."

"All right."

"Well, when?"

"I have to ask." Beth Ellen felt very vague.

"Well, *ask!*" Harriet seemed, sometimes, to be losing patience.

"Okay." Beth Ellen put the phone down and ran to her grandmother's room. She opened the door a crack and saw that the room was dark. Her grandmother was asleep. She closed the door softly and ran all the way down to the kitchen. The cook was making lunch for the maid and the chauffeur.

"Can you take me to Harriet's?" she asked the chauffeur, who was behind the newspaper.

"You're not to leave before you speak to your grandmother," said the maid.

"Why?" Beth Ellen's eyes got very large.

"Something has *happened*," said the chauffeur, leaning around his paper with his face a wide grin full of teeth.

"What?"

"Never mind him," said the cook. "It's just that she has something to tell you and she wants to tell you right after her nap. She left word."

The last two words were ominous. Whenever her grandmother *left word* about anything it was serious. She turned abruptly and left the kitchen. She ran upstairs to the phone.

"I can't come," she said into the phone.

"Why?"

"I have to stay home. My grandmother wants to see me. Something has happened." Beth Ellen began to feel important.

"WHAT?" Harriet screeched into the phone. She couldn't bear to have things happen that she knew nothing about.

"I don't know."

"Well, when you find out, will you call me?"

"Yes."

"Okay. Well, so long."

"Wait! Harriet?"

"Yeah?"

"Listen, Harriet, I tried it. Remember you said I ought to try writing again? Well, I tried it and I hate it."

"What did you write?"

"A letter to myself."

"A *letter* is not *writing*," said Harriet sternly.

"Anyway, what did it say?"

"It's private."

"Well, what are you telling me about it for, stupid?"

"Because I thought I'd try again like you said but I hate it."

"Listen, Beth Ellen"—Harriet sounded very severe —"you'll have to find a profession sooner or later, you know."

"I don't want to work. I hate it."

"You have to do *something!* You can't just lie around."

"Why not?"

"You just *can't!*" Harriet really screamed this time.

"But I have to do something I *like!*" Beth Ellen felt frantic.

"*All right!*" Then Harriet seemed to calm down. "Don't worry, we'll think of something. Listen, by the way, does anybody at your house read the Bible?"

"Why?"

"WHY ARE YOU SO DENSE SOMETIMES?" Harriet's yell must have been heard in Kansas. She continued, patiently: "We have to find out if all these quotes are from the Bible and if they are, we're dealing with a religious fanatic. We have to know who to LOOK FOR!" Her voice got away with her again at the end.

"I'll ask," said Beth Ellen wearily.

"Okay. Good work. Now, call me right away when you know what your grandmother says."

"Okay," said Beth Ellen, thinking: That is absolutely none of Harriet Welsch's business what my grandmother says.

"Okay, good-bye."

"Good-bye."

Beth Ellen hung up the phone and looked around the room. It was all a dark blue and in the half light looked spooky. Everything was blue—the heavy, brocaded bedspread, the thick rug, the heavy drapes that were never drawn to let in the day. Her grandfather had been dead for seven years. She remembered him with a curious emotion. He had given her a quarter every time he had seen her, which was nice; but before he gave her the quarter, he always asked if she were head of her class at school. She would say Yes and get the quarter. Curious, because she hadn't been in school at the time, being only four. She had loved him.

She looked over at the niche in the wall. There was a small altar stand with a huge Bible sitting open on it. On the stand also were two candles and a little place to kneel. Over the altar, on the wall, was a small, delicate painting of the Virgin. Beth Ellen had wondered about this, and her grandmother had told her that the house had formerly belonged to Catho-

51

lics and that she had just left everything where it was because it was pretty.

Beth Ellen sat thinking about Catholics. What did it feel like to be a Catholic? Did you feel more than other people? Maybe prettier things. Maybe your head was filled with prettier things. She thought of being in church with her grandmother. She went over to the Bible and looked at the open page. Did her grandmother read the Bible? Yes, but not this one, one by her bed. Did the cook, the chauffeur, the maid? I don't know, she thought, and I don't really care. She noticed that the book was open to Psalms. She read a line: "O sing unto the Lord a new song." I wish I had a new one to sing, she thought. She suddenly became intensely bored and wanted to close the book. She didn't, however, for it was prettier open. The only person I like in the whole Bible is Jeremiah, she thought wearily.

She looked around. She went over and closed the door. Then she took from under the bed a book she liked much better. It was a book she was seldom without, and she hid it in this room because no one came in except to clean and they evidently never cleaned under the bed. She opened the door quietly, planning to take the book back to her room. She saw the maid coming out of her grandmother's room. The maid beckoned to her.

"Your grandmother's awake now," she said, smiling in a friendly way.

"All right," said Beth Ellen.

"Go in and talk to her," said the maid, still smiling in a conspiratorial way, and went down the stairs.

Beth Ellen waited until she was out of the way, then went back into the room and put the book back under the bed. Then she went and knocked on her grandmother's door. Mrs. Hansen's "Come in" rang out in a cheery way. It can't be too bad, thought Beth Ellen as she opened the door.

"Come in, darling, I've got some good news for you." Mrs. Hansen was sitting up in bed and looking cheerful. Beth Ellen stood by the bed. She noticed that the lines around her grandmother's eyes, the little lines, were purple. Will I have purple eyes when I get old, she thought.

"Guess what!" Her grandmother's eyes were shining.

Beth Ellen said nothing.

"Your mother's coming home!" Her grandmother let this out in a little treble of joy.

Beth Ellen stood frozen to the spot. She could think of nothing to say. Why would my mother come here, she thought; she hates America.

"She's leaving for Paris in the morning, and although she cannot tell me exactly when, she will fly

53

right on to New York after that. She says that Paris is terribly dead in the summer, so I don't imagine she'll stay long." Her grandmother had a great smile on her face and looked at her expectantly.

Beth Ellen could think of nothing to say. She sensed that she was expected to say something, so she said, "How do you know?"

Her grandmother's eyes widened. "Well, I know because she called me! She called me from Athens! Isn't that exciting?"

Beth Ellen just stood, feeling stupid. Was it excitement she felt? She didn't know what to feel. She remembered her mother as a whitish blur in a large white hat.

"It's typical of Zeeney not to be able to say when she would arrive. She has hated being pinned down since she was a tiny child. I imagine that's why she's never been able to stay in one place for long. But it doesn't matter, does it? It's brought me the most adorable child in the world. But just think! You haven't seen your mother since your grandfather's death, since you were five years old! This must be the most exciting thing in the world for you!" Mrs. Hansen delivered this with great enthusiasm, then looked quizzically at Beth Ellen.

Beth Ellen suddenly felt like running, crying, laughing, scratching, screaming, and jumping out the window all at the same time. She also felt nailed to the floor. If she could only get out of the room, away from that stare, and take this piece of news, squirrel-like, to her room.

"Grandmother, I'll be right back. I forgot to finish something that I was doing." She held her breath.

"Oh, my poor darling. Come here. Come here to your grandmother." Mrs. Hansen held out her arms.

This was awful, the worst that could happen. Beth Ellen's heart leapt in terror. If she holds me, if she hugs me, if she says one word, I will drown in tears. She ran from the room. She ran as fast as she could down the hall. She heard her grandmother call but she knew she wouldn't come after her so she ran into her room and shut the door.

She stood with one hand on the doorknob, looking at it. The knob was made of brass and it was carved. She stared at the carving which twisted its convoluted way around the long, cylindric handle.

She went and sat on the edge of the bed. My mother, she thought, and then, experimentally, "Mother." She said it aloud. "Mother." It came like a soft purr into the silent room.

No. Nothing. She felt nothing. What was there to feel? What was one supposed to feel? Her grandmother had used the word "exciting." That was when something nice would happen. Or spying with Harriet, like the other day, that was exciting. She didn't feel excited. This was not excitement. It felt more like an ache. Like a tooth feels right before it's *going* to ache. Not when it had started, because then it hurt. She didn't hurt. She just felt rather limp and . . . sensitive.

She tried to remember everything she could about her mother. The large white blur, the big white hat, the orchid . . . oh, yes, she had forgotten the orchid. . . . Why an orchid? . . . Wallace . . . there she felt something. . . . She would finally meet Wallace . . . the Wallace of all the letters . . . the Wallace this and Wallace that . . . and the photographs of her mother, a long, tall beautiful woman . . . and Wallace, a thin, handsome blond man . . . in ski clothes . . . on a beach . . . holding drinks at a party . . . leaving on a boat . . . leaving on a plane . . . going somewhere on horses . . . on camels . . . on elephants.

Beth Ellen had seen each picture as it arrived. Her grandmother had offered to give her some so that she might look at them alone in her room, but she had said No politely and wondered to herself, What for? They were two strangers who by now looked familiar, the way it is when you think you know someone on the street and then you realize he is only a movie star.

So now the photographs would move. She thought of them almost as dolls that one dressed up. They had riding clothes, swimming clothes, street clothes, evening clothes, and when she saw them they would have on traveling clothes complete in every detail. Or perhaps country clothes, since they were coming to Water Mill. Wallace would have on tweeds . . . no, it was summer.

She felt exhausted suddenly. Try as she might she could not find one emotion connected with this piece of news. She lay back on the bed. She felt the bedspread. It was nice to feel something with her hands, something solid. Was her mother coming to take her away, like something she had bought at a dress shop and couldn't wait to have delivered? Would her grandmother let them take her? Did her grandmother want her to go? Where do I live, she thought, and began to cry. She cried a long time, then fell asleep, her face lying in a wet patch of tears.

An hour must have passed before there was a knock on her door. She got up and opened the door. It was the maid.

"Mrs. Hansen said you're to come to her room." She looked curiously at Beth Ellen.

"All right," said Beth Ellen, then as she turned away, "Thank you."

"You're welcome, sweetheart," said the maid and swished away down the hall.

Beth Ellen felt numb. She remembered everything. She went into the bathroom and washed her face. Then she marched herself out and down the hall to her grandmother's room. She knocked on the door. When she heard her grandmother's voice, she opened the door with what was, for Beth Ellen, great determination.

"There, darling, did you finish your little project?"

"Yes."

"Sit down and tell me what you feel about your mother coming."

Beth Ellen sat down and looked at her grandmother. There was a gleam of something close to defiance in her round, blue eyes.

Her grandmother didn't seem to notice. "Isn't it just the *most* exciting thing? To think that not only are you going to see your mother, but I'm going to see my daughter after seven years! I *do* enjoy her, in short doses of course. And Wallace! *I've* never met *Wallace!* Your mother says that he's enchanting! Isn't it enthralling, the whole thing?"

"No."

"What, darling?"

"No."

"No, what?"

"No, it isn't exciting."

"Why, what do you mean, dear?"

"It isn't exciting to me."

"Why, what are you talking about? Of course it is. It's the most exciting moment of your young life, I should imagine. If *I* were to have seen my mother

58

after seven years, *I* would have been *terribly* excited, so I *know* what you *must* feel."

"Nothing."

"What?"

"I don't feel anything."

"Why, that's ridiculous. Of course you do."

"I do not." Beth Ellen's voice had an edge to it that she hadn't exactly planned on. She felt a little startled herself at what she was doing. Still, was she wrong in feeling that her grandmother seemed a little pleased under all her reactions of surprise?

"Beth Ellen Hansen! What in the world is in your mind?"

"Nothing."

"You come over here this minute and let me look at you. I can't see that far."

Beth Ellen stood up obediently and walked over to the side of the bed.

"You've been crying," her grandmother said in astonishment.

"I have not."

"Yes, you have. There's nothing wrong with crying. Why would you lie about it? I'm rather glad to see you have some emotion about it." Her grandmother said this, but she didn't look at all glad about it. "I wouldn't want you to act that way in front of your mother when she's here. She has a tricky mind, your mother. She would think I had turned you against her

59

in some tricky way. I don't suppose you remember her well enough to remember that sort of thing, do you?"

Beth Ellen shook her head. She was glad the conversation had shifted away from her onto her mother. What *was* her mother like? What kind of person?

As though in answer, her grandmother began to talk.

"She is a vital woman, your mother, a startlingly beautiful, vibrant, *most* exciting woman. She can turn a roomful of intelligent men into babbling idiots within a few seconds upon entering. But her mind is quixotic, volatile, takes great unknown leaps into curious bypaths. Wallace, I suspect, is one such path."

Mrs. Hansen said this last looking toward the window and rather as though Beth Ellen were not in the room.

"Your father, of course, was a different matter. Rather stern, but an immensely likable fellow. Never said much. Never said a word, in fact, the morning he left—just got up, packed a bag, and left forever."

Beth Ellen rather liked that. Her father, at least, seemed a sensible sort.

"But your mother was wild, is wild, and always will *be* wild. She is a strange, extravagant person, one to be admired for some things and avoided for others. Nervous too, high-strung like a horse."

Beth Ellen saw a horse in a big, white picture hat.

"You will like her, I'm sure." Her grandmother

looked doubtfully at Beth Ellen. "Well, perhaps 'like' is not the right word. But you will admire her. Of that I am sure." Mrs. Hansen smiled and her eyes twinkled reassuringly.

Beth Ellen wasn't at all sure about anything. What kind of a mother was this? She sounded as if she danced a lot.

"She loves to have a good time. I've never quite understood that because nothing ever seemed much like a good time to me. There are good times in life, but *a good time* is something else. To your mother, however, almost everything except serious thinking and serious people can be considered a good time."

Am I a serious person, thought Beth Ellen hastily.

"Your father, I'm afraid, fell into the category of a serious person. Only because he accomplished things. Your mother has a tremendous appetite for doing nothing whatsoever. She never *ever*, from the time she was a little child, wanted to do anything but marry a rich man and have a good time. So she married your father, and of course now . . . Wallace."

"Why do I have your name and not my father's?" Beth Ellen asked suddenly. She wondered why it had never occurred to her to ask this question before.

"Because your mother was so livid when your father left that she had your name changed. A rich man who leaves and spoils your good time is naturally no good whatever."

Beth Ellen thought of what she had said to Harriet on the beach. "I must call Harriet," she said.

"Of course; call her at once. You want to tell her your mother is coming, don't you? Run along, dear, and I'll see you at dinner. Perhaps we'll look over some of the photographs then. It's rather hard for *me* to remember what Zeeney looks like."

Beth Ellen closed the door behind her, then stopped short. Zeeney? Oh, yes, that was her mother's name. She ran to the phone.

"Hello," Harriet answered. When it was raining she sat by the phone to intercept any news.

"It's me. Beth Ellen."

"I know it. What happened?"

"My mother's coming home."

"WHAAAT?"

"They're coming home."

"Who's *they?*"

"My mother, Zeeney, and Wallace."

"Your mother WHAT?" screamed Harriet.

"That's her *name*. Zeeney," said Beth Ellen patiently.

"Who's Wallace?"

"Her husband."

"When?" Harriet was practically gasping she was so excited.

"I don't know. She doesn't tell things like that. She just appears," said Beth Ellen importantly.

"WOW."

At least Harriet was having a satisfactory reaction. Beth Ellen was silent because she was thinking that Harriet always said "Wow." Then she thought a long time about "Wow."

"Hello, hello, are you there?" Harriet screamed into the phone as though it were a transatlantic cable.

"Yes."

"Well, when can *I* see them? Can I see them right away? What do they look like? Do you like them? I never knew you even *had* any parents. You don't have any parents. Listen, Beth Ellen, I've known you since kindergarten and you don't *have* any parents. What *is* this?"

"I have a mother and she's coming here."

"I never knew that. I didn't know that at all. I thought your mother was . . ." Harriet stopped spewing and trailed off.

"What?" asked Beth Ellen, interested for the first time.

"I don't know. I mean, I just thought she wasn't around."

"She *wasn't*."

"Well, why don't you tell me some more. When can I see them?"

"I don't know. When they get here, I guess. There isn't any more to tell."

"Listen, Beth Ellen"—Harriet's voice dropped to a whisper—"I've got something to tell *you!*"

"What?" said Beth Ellen, expecting a lecture.

"That Jessie Mae Jenkins is, this very minute, in the *filling station!*"

"So?"

"Well, she has to be there an hour, getting her bike fixed, so I went over to her house and I saw something in the garage you wouldn't *believe!*"

"What?"

"I can't tell you, I have to show you. Can you come out?"

"It's raining."

"No, it isn't. It's stopped raining. Haven't you noticed? What do you think? I've been riding around out there dripping wet?"

"Oh."

"Listen, come on. Meet me at the filling station. I have an idea."

Beth Ellen thought a minute of the coolish late afternoon air on her face as she rode along and said, "Yes. All right, I'll meet you."

"Okay. In five minutes. Better make it at the post office. We don't want to arouse her suspicions," said Harriet.

Beth Ellen hung up the phone and ran out of the room. She grabbed a sweater and ran out of the house without saying anything to anybody.

CHAPTER 7

Harriet was standing by the post office. When Beth Ellen came up, Harriet whispered, "Now's our chance."

"For what?" said Beth Ellen.

"To *talk* to her!" said Harriet, rolling her bike toward the filling station. As she rolled her bike a hideous noise issued from the underpart.

"What's the matter with your bike?" asked Beth Ellen. Beth Ellen had one of those bikes that was continually breaking down, so that she had spent most of last summer in the filling station, but she had

65

never known anything to go wrong with Harriet's.

"I broke it," whispered Harriet, "so we'd have a reason to go in there."

"Oh," said Beth Ellen, marveling.

They pushed their bikes into the station. There was Jessie Mae sitting on a curb chewing a leaf. She looked at them with veiled curiosity.

The bike man nodded to Beth Ellen and went to her bike, but Harriet said, "It's mine!"

He bent down and examined the damage. "How did this happen?" he asked.

"I can't imagine," said Harriet and looked at the highway.

"Well, it'll take about an hour," said the man.

"An HOUR," said Harriet. "What kind of SERVICE do you get here?" She dwindled down at the last because the bike man looked as if he might throw the bike at her.

"An hour," he said briefly, and picking up the bike in one hand, he went into the station.

They stood there a minute after he left. Harriet looked slanty-eyed at Jessie Mae. "Let's go," she said finally to Beth Ellen.

Beth Ellen wasn't at all sure what they were doing, but she followed dutifully as Harriet sauntered over to Jessie Mae.

"Hi," said Harriet.

Jessie Mae looked up and moved the leaf to one side of her mouth. "Hi, y'all," she said.

"Is your bike broken too?" asked Harriet.

"Yeah. It's most always broke," said Jessie Mae.

"So is mine," said Beth Ellen, but Harriet looked at her as though to say: I am in charge of this investigation.

"Well," said Jessie Mae, "I'm Jessie Mae Jenkins, and we might as well talk a little while. What's y'all's names?"

"WHAT?" said Harriet, who couldn't understand a word.

"What y'all called?" said Jessie Mae.

"Beth Ellen Hansen," said Beth Ellen.

"*Oh!*" said Harriet. "Harriet M. Welsch."

"How do," said Jessie Mae and moved over a little so they could sit down. Beth Ellen leaned her bike, then sat, but Harriet continued to stand so she could stare at Jessie Mae. If Jessie Mae felt those eyes boring into her, she showed no sign of it. "Mighty hot, ain't it?" she said in a friendly way.

It wasn't, as a matter of fact, hot at all this late in the day, but Beth Ellen knew she meant it had *been* hot, so she said, "Yes."

"What are you talking about, Beth Ellen? It isn't at all hot," said Harriet, beginning to feel left out because she could hardly understand Jessie Mae at all.

Jessie Mae looked at Harriet as though she were a tree stump and said brightly to Beth Ellen, "Liked to turn into a grease spot this morning in that kitchen. Over to the house you could fry nice couple eggs on the sidewalk," and she nodded sagely.

Beth Ellen felt she should make up in politeness what Harriet was losing in rudeness, so she said sweetly, "Where do you live?"

"Why, goodness gracious," said Jessie Mae, cool as a cucumber, "y'all ought to know, seeing as how you been looking in the window." She picked up a comic book from the curb next to her and fanned herself.

Beth Ellen turned red and looked at Harriet for help. Harriet yawned. She had decided to bide her time to see what attitude Jessie Mae took on the subject. Jessie Mae looked at the yawn.

"Ain't that right, fatty?" she said cheerfully and poked Harriet with the rolled-up comic book.

"I'm NOT FAT!" said Harriet loudly.

Jessie Mae let out a high giggle and looked at Beth Ellen, who laughed outright.

"Stop that!" said Harriet to Beth Ellen, who was so shocked she stopped immediately.

"You the captain and she the lieutenant?" said Jessie Mae, beside herself with giggles.

Beth Ellen started to laugh again too, and they both looked at Harriet and laughed even harder.

"*Well!*" said Harriet, but she could think of nothing else, so she sat down abruptly. She decided to brazen it out.

"How's the watermelon business?" she said lightly.

Jessie Mae fanned herself busily. "Why, my goodness, we just pulling in the money. Right now we doing the work here, but later on we gonna move to the city and there'll be lots of people working for us and we'll have lots of money." Jessie Mae fanned herself a lot and looked proud. "The Lord willing," she added. "I got to get back, s'matter of fact, soon as my bike's done. We got a lot of work today because all the melons arrived."

"I know," said Harriet.

"You been over there again?" Jessie Mae looked at her in surprise. "Shoot, girl, why don't y'all come on home with me? I'll show you all you want to see. Y'all don't have to sneak around like that."

Harriet's eyes opened wide. Beth Ellen said politely, "Thank you so much."

"Nothing to it," said Jessie Mae, fanning. "Mama'll be glad for some company. I seen you two around a lot. I did wonder why I didn't see you in Sunday school."

"SUNDAY SCHOOL?" Harriet's voice came out in a croak.

"I go to Sunday school in New York," said Beth Ellen hastily, "but in the summer, I just go to church with my grandmother."

"Oh?" said Jessie Mae with interest. "What church?"

69

"Episcopal."

"I go the Methodist," said Jessie Mae.

"You never told me that, Beth Ellen," shouted Harriet. "You don't go to Sunday school. What are you saying?"

"I do so," said Beth Ellen.

"Well, I don't," said Harriet. "What's it like?"

"It's interesting," said Jessie Mae. "You ought to come sometime with me. You'd like it. You mean to tell me"—Jessie Mae's voice went up a register—"that you don't go to church *or* Sunday school? You have Bible school in the city?"

"BIBLE?" screeched Harriet.

"Yes. You know, study the Book and all that?"

"No." Harriet narrowed her eyes. "Why?" she said seductively.

"Well, I wondered. I am particularly interested, seeing as how I plans to be a preacher and all." She looked intently back at Harriet.

"You DOES . . . I mean, you DO?"

"Well, what's the matter with that, Harriet?" Beth Ellen spoke up. "If she wants to be a preacher, let her be a preacher."

"There ain't a whole lot she can do about it," said Jessie Mae and grinned.

"*I* am going to be a *wife!*" said Beth Ellen.

"Oh, Beth Ellen, please," said Harriet in disgust.

Jessie Mae laughed. "Why, I think that's just lovely. What's wrong with being a wife? What you gonna be, fatty, an astronaut?"

"Now, that's going TOO FAR!" yelled Harriet.

Beth Ellen began to like Jessie Mae. With her tinkling voice she seemed to be able to say the most devastating things to Harriet, the kind of things that Beth Ellen only thought of later, on her way home, when it was too late.

"I plans to be a wife too. What's wrong with that?" Jessie Mae looked at Harriet with an amused glint in her eyes as though she were ready to let loose a cascade of giggles.

"NOTHING!" Harriet began to splutter. "But you can't just lie around being a wife. . . . That's all she wants to do"—she pointed at Beth Ellen—"just lie around all day doing nothing but being a wife. All I *mean* is you ought to do something *too;* like my friend Janie is going to be a scientist and my friend Sport is going to be a ball player and I'm going to be a writer and you're going to be a preacher." Harriet thought herself inordinately clever for inserting the last.

Beth Ellen felt suddenly depressed. She wanted to get away from them. She stood up and started to walk toward the station.

"Where you *going?*" Harriet called after her.

"Where do you *think* I'm going, *Harriet?*" yelled Beth Ellen with great irritation and disappeared inside. Having gotten the key from the man, she came out again and disappeared around the building.

Harriet and Jessie Mae sat in silence for a while. Jessie Mae fanned herself.

She turned suddenly and looked at Harriet. "If I may say so, you do speak sharply to your friend."

"She's MY friend," said Harriet appalled.

"Well . . ." said Jessie Mae, looking away and fanning rapidly, "I do feel that, like the Good Book says, we should honor our father and mother, but I, personally, think we should honor our friends too."

Harriet was stunned into silence. They sat a little longer this way, the only noise being the swish-swish of Jessie Mae's fan. Harriet was thinking rapidly. She finally said to Jessie Mae, "How does one go about being a preacher?"

"Well," said Jessie Mae, "it's not all that easy, specially for a woman, but I'm studying on how with a man I know."

"Who's that?" said Harriet.

"A man live right over there named The Preacher. I goes to his place and we has long talks. He knows a lot of things."

"You mean that old Negro man that lives out in the woods?" Harriet was amazed. The Preacher was a familiar sight in Water Mill.

"He knows a whole lot of things," said Jessie Mae, fanning furiously.

"What things?" Harriet was now completely fascinated.

"Oh, he knows the Book backwards and forwards. Every year he reads it over again, starting at Genesis and going right on through." Jessie Mae was very impressed. Harriet wasn't.

"Doesn't he have anything else to read? Why doesn't he go to the library?"

"Why, he don't *have* to! Don't you know that?" Jessie Mae asked in a syrupy voice. "Everything is in the Good Book. You just have to find it. When you read it as much as he do, well, he done found just about everything there is to find."

"Do you read it?" asked Harriet slyly.

"Oh, yes," said Jessie Mae, "every night and every morning."

"You talk funny," said Harriet abruptly. She didn't mean to be mean. It had just suddenly occurred to her and so she said it.

"So do you, Yankee girl," sang out Jessie Mae, completely unperturbed.

Beth Ellen had been walking over to them and now she sat down again.

"I was just about to do that very thing," said Jessie Mae, and getting up, she went in and got the key and disappeared around the building.

73

"Listen, Beth Ellen," said Harriet wildly, grabbing Beth Ellen's arm as soon as Jessie Mae was out of earshot, "we've got her!"

"Who?" said Beth Ellen.

"It's her!" said Harriet, bubbling with laughter. "Now I'm sure of it." When she saw Beth Ellen looking blank, she said, "The note leaver! It's her. She reads the Bible all the time. She's learning how to be a preacher from that man called The Preacher, and he does *nothing* but read the Bible!" Harriet was triumphant.

"Maybe it's him, then," said Beth Ellen.

Harriet looked at her in a stunned way. She slapped her forehead with her hand, said, "I never *thought* of that!" and looked at Beth Ellen with admiration.

"Our bikes are ready," Beth Ellen said coolly and got up, leaving Harriet staring at her. She walked toward the station. Harriet M. Welsch doesn't know everything in the world, she thought as she walked along. Jessie Mae had come back and was paying for her bike. Harriet ran up.

The man wheeled Harriet's bike out. "I don't have any money. You have to charge it," said Harriet importantly.

Beth Ellen rolled her bike over. Jessie Mae was leaning down, examining her bike minutely. She looked into the basket in the front. "Why, looky here!" she said in a high voice. "What's this?"

Harriet and Beth Ellen looked over her shoulder. In the bottom of the basket lay a piece of paper.

HE THAT IS WITHOUT SIN AMONG YOU
LET HIM FIRST CAST A STONE AT YOU

"Why, how in the sam hill did that get in there?" said Jessie Mae in a terribly high voice.

Hmmmmmm, thought Harriet, could she have put that in her own bike so she wouldn't be suspected?

The garage man looked too. "Those things are all over the place. I got two of them already. Nobody knows who's doing it. I hear everybody in Water Mill has gone to the police about it, and they can't find out anything either. It's pretty funny. We never had anything like this before in Water Mill."

"What did the police do?" asked Harriet, watching Jessie Mae's face carefully.

"What can they do?" asked the garage man and shrugged. "It's not really breaking any law. It's just annoying to people, kind of a nuisance." He twitched a little. "They kinda hit home too, some of these things."

"Could I see the ones you got?" asked Harriet, feeling very important and rather Sherlock Holmes.

He laughed. "Well, sure, if you want to. I don't

know if they're still around. You can if they're here."
He went inside.

"Well, I don't understand. This here is about a fancy woman."

"A what?" said Harriet.

"A whore," said Beth Ellen.

Harriet turned on Jessie Mae, her voice dripping with suspicion. "How do *you* know that?"

"Why, anybody knows that," said Jessie Mae. "Anybody goes to Sunday school, that is." And she looked at Beth Ellen and laughed. She and Beth Ellen laughed together as though they shared a secret. Harriet looked offended.

"But it could just mean some people are being mean to you," said Beth Ellen to Jessie Mae.

"That's a fact," said Jessie Mae.

"Hhrumph," said Harriet, too grumpy to speak.

The garage man came out with two pieces of paper in his hand and gave them to Harriet. "Give 'em back, though," he said. "Police might want 'em sometime." He went to wait on a customer.

Harriet shifted through them, with Jessie Mae and Beth Ellen looking over her shoulder:

NOW BARABBAS WAS A ROBBER

was the first one. Then:

"I get the feeling," said Harriet, "that this garage cheats you."

"My heavens," said Jessie Mae, "whoever wrote those sure does know his Bible, *mmmm, mmmmm.*"

She could, thought Harriet, be patting herself on the back.

"Listen, Jessie Mae," said Harriet in a whisper, "you want to help us catch this note leaver?" I'm very crafty, thought Harriet. If she's the note leaver, she'll say No.

"Well!" said Jessie Mae, laughing, "I don't know but what he's doing a whole lot of good in the world. Don't hurt people none to get a touch of the Bible!"

Harriet narrowed her eyes. The garage man came over. "Funny, aren't they? You'd think I was a crook the way they sound. That's what everybody is going to the police about. These things make you sound terrible."

Harriet was looking at him so slitty-eyed she could hardly see. She handed the notes back. "Perhaps he won't be around long," she said pointedly. The garage man looked a little startled but didn't answer.

"Let's go on to my house, all right?" Jessie Mae cried gaily as she jumped on her bike.

"Sure," said Beth Ellen and got on hers.

Jessie Mae started off and Beth Ellen followed, then Harriet pumping along like a hound dog on the scent.

CHAPTER 8

They hardly spoke on the way to the Jenkins' house. Jessie Mae rode very fast, and Harriet tried to keep up.

Beth Ellen was too filled with dark thoughts to want to talk. Riding her bike in the cool air made her forget the garage and think only of the scene with her grandmother. She began to turn over and over in her mind the phrase, I will not think about it. I will not think about the word *Mother*. As they pulled up in front of the house she thought: Mother—whatever that is.

They rode right into the driveway this time. Harriet said, "Hurry up, Beth Ellen. I can't wait," and streaked after Jessie Mae. Beth Ellen hurried. Hurrying after Harriet made her feel curiously liberated, as though she could be a child and it was all right. Harriet always gave her this feeling. It was one of the few things she *really* liked about Harriet, as a matter of fact, because the principal feeling she felt when with Harriet was one of being continually jarred.

At the end of the driveway they scorched to a stop in front of a curious scene. Through the corridor formed by an immense pile of watermelons lining both sides of the driveway they could see into the open garage at the end. Mama Jenkins, taking up the space of three witches, her face a glowing red ball, sweat dripping down all over her black dress, stood stirring an enormous boiling vat which stood on a base over a raging fire. In this was an erupting concoction from which issued a pungent but not altogether unpleasant, yet too harsh, smell which smashed into their faces with every gust of smoke from the pot. There was an old tennis shoe smell, then a sweet smell as of a fresh orange, then just a touch of something that could have been creosote. Each time the smoke came in their direction they had to hold their noses and not breathe until it veered away again.

Mama Jenkins was, inexplicably, shouting. It was hard to know why, because she was all alone, unless perhaps it was just part of her routine when she stirred the pot.

"Hail, hail there, come on with the business, get it made, get it boiled, get it bottled, get it shipped, get the loot, for the glory of the Lord God in the highest. Hey there, come on outchere with those watermelonssssss." Then she saw them. "Hello there, little helpers. Bless your soul, Jessie Mae, you brought some help. I can't get those two to do nothing!" Then she shouted toward the house again: "Hey there, hey there, hey there, more and more and more. Norman, come a-running. Magnolia, come a-running; get yourself here; get yourself *outchere*. . . ." Then suddenly the rhythm broke and Mama Jenkins, with both feet planted a mile apart, really yelled, "OUT-CHERE RIGHT THIS RED HOT MINUTE!"

The back door burst open and like two helpful dwarfs Norman and Magnolia catapulted through the door and shot toward the garage. As Jessie Mae was putting her bike away they started to work furiously. Without saying a word they each picked up a watermelon, which was not easy for either one of them but for Magnolia was an insoluble problem. She got it up to somewhere near her knees, and it just stayed there while she hung on for dear life and looked around helplessly. Norman picked his up with only a short pig-noise of effort, wobbled to the vat, and with one heave threw it in. Mama Jenkins stepped back artfully so as not to be covered by the wave of goo which shot straight up and splashed down again.

"Keep 'em coming, keep 'em coming, keep 'em coming," she yelled like a carnival barker. Jessie Mae grabbed one now and pushed it in, her face red with the strain and her thin arms roped with thin muscles. "We gonna get rich, we gonna get richer, we gonna get richest!" Mama Jenkins sang as she hopped around, avoiding Jessie Mae's splash. Norman ran to Magnolia, who was still standing glued to the floor, her eyes bulging. He picked up her watermelon and threw it in the pot. Magnolia fell over.

As she watched Mama Jenkins hopping around, Beth Ellen was reminded of a delicate hippo she had once seen at the zoo. The hippo had stepped daintily out of her bath of sludge, and putting her head back, had seemed to laugh and call out some witticism to her mate. At the time Beth Ellen had thought it sweet, had wondered what it would be like to be a hippo and be married to a hippo. At least one wouldn't be lonely. Mama Jenkins' singing now filled her with the same feeling. It must be nice to be Jessie Mae and live here.

"I got to work now, y'all, I'm sorry. I see you tomorrow," said Jessie Mae, suddenly remembering them.

"Let them come on and work too," said Mama Jenkins jovially. "Won't do them no harm and might do some good."

"But they my *friends,* Mama! They come for a visit. They shouldn't have to *work!*" Jessie Mae stood aghast, holding a watermelon and looking at Mama Jenkins as though she might burst into tears.

"Well, that's true," said Mama Jenkins cheerfully. "Y'all come back one day before we start to work, and I'll give you a lemonade and some homemade cookies." She smiled a beautiful hippo smile, and Harriet and Beth Ellen smiled back without even being aware of it.

"I'll see y'all, hear?" said Jessie Mae and waved.

They said, "Okay," and wheeled their bikes down the driveway.

When they got to the road they looked back. It was impossible to tell from the front of the house what an extraordinary scene was taking place in the back. Only an occasional sour wisp of smoke gave any indication. Harriet began to get on her bike.

"Maybe we should have helped," said Beth Ellen.

"What?" said Harriet. "Imagine picking up all those things. We might break our backs, or our toes, or heaven knows what all you could break. . . ."

Harriet looked so outraged that Beth Ellen began to laugh.

"What are you laughing at, Beth Ellen? It seems to me that I've been awfully funny today, a regular barrel of laughs. I don't see . . ." Beth Ellen was laughing on and on, when suddenly a deep voice like a cello boomed over their shoulders.

"And what, might I ask, is so amusing to two very rich little summer residents?"

They turned, stricken, to realize they were looking into the long, brown horseface of The Preacher.

They looked up at him open-mouthed. He was a very long tall man. His face was almost as long as his vest. He looked like a chocolate-covered basset hound.

"Do you not have tongues?" he intoned mirthlessly. There was, however, a shine in his yellow eyes, and his cheeks looked less forlorn for a moment.

"Well," said Harriet, "what?" Which wasn't very clever, but understandable under the circumstances.

"What makes you merry, little rich critters? Will you enter the kingdom of heaven?"

"Certainly," said Harriet without a pause.

Beth Ellen felt a certain terror. The Preacher and Harriet were looking at each other as though they might enter into hand-to-hand combat.

"You are sure of yourself." He spoke slowly, thoughtfully, as though gauging Harriet.

Harriet seemed a little taken aback by this but stood her ground and did not blink an eyelash.

"Do you know the perils of undue curiosity?" He spoke fiercely.

Beth Ellen felt frightened again, but only for a

moment, because she heard Harriet yell in that way that only Harriet could yell.

"LISTEN HERE, YOU! WHAT ARE YOU TALKING ABOUT?" Harriet was so angry she looked like a red lollipop. Beth Ellen whirled quickly to look at The Preacher.

He smiled a very slow, very mysterious smile, then he turned. He twirled his walking stick and with a quick step, almost a vaudeville turn, he sashayed into the road. He looked back once as he walked on his jaunty way, smiled again, then began to whistle. It sounded to Beth Ellen like the kind of tune one would hear in an Italian movie.

She looked at Harriet, but Harriet, for once, was speechless. She was staring in the same way Beth Ellen had been staring. They watched the strange, almost but not quite comic figure that walked, almost but not quite danced, down the road.

When they turned to look at each other it was as though the world were suddenly quiet, very quiet. It was as though there had been an unearthly visitation.

"Well," said Harriet. Beth Ellen said nothing but looked at Harriet in an effort to get some clue as to how to behave. Harriet didn't have a clue. She stood with one foot on her bike, then looked down as though she would push off, then stopped and looked again up the road. The Preacher was a small black shadow-figure now, a doll in the flat landscape.

Beth Ellen got on her bike and began to wobble off down the road. When she remembered what she was going back to, dinner with her grandmother and more discussions of Zeeney, she felt a sudden fall in her stomach. The feeling made her lose her footing and she had to put her foot out so she wouldn't fall over. She stood with one foot on the ground and looked back at Harriet. Harriet stood still, hypnotized, looking after the dot of a man.

"Let's go," said Beth Ellen, beginning to feel uneasy in the darkening air.

Harriet rolled her bike over. "You know," she said, never taking her eyes off The Preacher, "he knows too much. I don't like this one bit." She leaned her bike against her stomach and there, in the middle of the road, she took out her notebook and made a few notes.

With all her spying, thought Beth Ellen, she hates it if someone spies on her. How odd she is, anyway. What possible fun could it be to write everything down all the time? So tiresome.

Harriet slammed her book closed and put it away. She got on her bike and pushed ahead. Beth Ellen followed. Actually, she thought, considering what I'm going home to, this spying around isn't bad at all. She looked at Harriet pumping away ahead of her and felt affectionate.

CHAPTER 9

The next day Beth Ellen woke up feeling terrible. As she lay there she thought to herself that she had been feeling bad for two days. She had felt like just sitting around. She had also felt fat. Maybe I rode too far on the bike yesterday, she thought. No, I feel worse than that. I feel awful. She said aloud to herself, "I feel bad."

She sat up. She moved aside and looked at the bed sheet. She felt frightened. I'm sick, she thought. She looked around the room as though for help. She got up and went into the bathroom.

When she came out she was dressed. She walked down the steps through the quiet, dark house. She felt extremely odd. She walked through the living room, through the sun room, and out onto the back lawn.

Feeling as though she might faint, she walked slowly—although she wanted to run because she wanted to hide—to the summerhouse, which was protected from view by a row of boxwood. Once inside the hedge she felt safe. She walked into the play of light and shade inside the summerhouse and curled onto a wicker chaise.

She lay back watching the leaves above her head, the black-green curling leaves against the thin blue of the summer sky. The place smelled of summers, of Victorian afternoons, and of a gentle luxury. She sank deep into the cushions.

She stayed there all day, past the cook's call to lunch, past several calls to the phone, into the late afternoon.

She didn't think as she lay there, just let the leaves, the alternating cool of the shade and heat, as a ray of sun escaped the leaves and warmed her face, wash over her, fill her with hope. It was all a mistake. She would get up, go inside, and know it was all a dream.

As the day began to cool, the shadows of the hedges lengthen, the maid came across the lawn calling. Beth Ellen didn't answer, but she knew she would be found. It was her favorite place to cry and the servants knew.

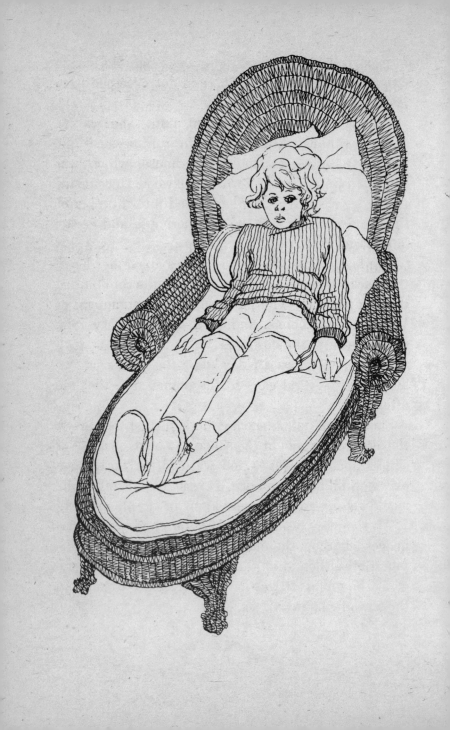

The maid appeared around the hedge. "Why didn't you answer?"

"I was asleep," said Beth Ellen, and her voice came out in a croak because she hadn't spoken all day.

"Your grandmother wants to see you," said the maid.

Beth Ellen stood up, feeling like an old woman. She followed the maid across the lawn, the shadows dark now and cold.

Harriet called up just as Beth Ellen came out of her grandmother's room.

"Hey!"

"Harriet?" whispered Beth Ellen. She felt as though she'd just come out of a bomb shelter.

"Who'd you expect—Mary Poppins?" yelled Harriet and then flooded Beth Ellen's ear with raucous, endless laughter.

"Mmm," murmured Beth Ellen, feeling lost. I'm all alone, she thought.

"Listen, Mouse," continued Harriet, regaining her voice, "good news. Janie's coming for the weekend!"

"Mmm," said Beth Ellen, hearing *Janie* as a remote, pleasant word.

"Isn't that *great?*" Harriet seemed to be trying to yell her way through Beth Ellen's vagueness. "She's coming out tonight with my dad and staying till Sunday!"

"Mmm," said Beth Ellen.

"MOUSE!" Harriet gave one great agonized yelp.

"What?" whispered Beth Ellen.

"WHAT'S WRONG WITH YOU?"

"I'm—"

"WHAT?"

Beth Ellen's voice suddenly found itself and came out so loud she jumped. "I'm—menstruating!"

"What's that?" asked Harriet, awed.

"It's—"

"I just remembered," yelled Harriet. "How come you're doing that and I'm not?"

It was an unanswerable question. "I don't know—" began Beth Ellen.

Harriet hung up on her.

The next day was Saturday and Beth Ellen went to Harriet's house for the day. When she came into the bedroom, Harriet and Janie were discussing the situation.

"I've been working on a cure for this thing ever since it happened to me," Janie said, frowning and looking very serious, even though she was lying upside down on the bed in a bathing suit with her feet straight up against the wall.

"What kind of cure?" asked Harriet, after she had said Hello to Beth Ellen.

"I just want to *end* it, that's all," said Janie in a furious way.

"But . . . doesn't it have something to do with babies?" asked Harriet.

"How would you know, Harriet Welsch? You haven't even done it," snarled Janie, swinging her legs down to the floor and sitting up. "You wouldn't know a Fallopian tube if you fell over one."

Chagrined, Harriet pointed to Beth Ellen. *"She's* done it; yesterday. She told me."

Beth Ellen turned bright red, looked at the floor, and wanted to die. They both stared at her.

Janie finally spoke, and softly, "What's there to think about? It's a nuisance, that's all, and frankly, I think, should be done away with."

Beth Ellen kept looking at the floor.

"What's it feel like?" asked Harriet.

"Yuuuuuchk," said Janie. "It has absolutely nothing to recommend it." She looked at Beth Ellen as she continued. "You don't feel like working or playing or anything but just lying around and looking at the ceiling, right? Icky. Right, Mouse?"

Beth Ellen nodded but still couldn't look up for some reason.

Janie looked at her a minute, then said, "It happens to everybody, though, every woman in the world, even Madame Curie. It's very normal. And I guess, since it means you're grown up and can have babies, that it's a good thing. I, for one, just don't happen to want babies. I also have a sneaking suspicion that there're too many babies in the world already. So I'm working on this cure for people that don't want babies, so they won't have to do this."

Beth Ellen looked up at Janie and asked tentatively, "Do those rocks hurt you too?"

"*Rocks?*" Janie yelled.

"Those rocks inside that come down," said Beth Ellen timidly.

"WHAT?" screamed Harriet. "Oh, well, if they think I'm gonna do anything like that, they're crazy."

"There aren't any rocks. Who *told* you that?" Janie was so mad she stood up. "Who told you there were rocks? There aren't any rocks. I'll kill 'em. Who told you that about any rocks?"

Beth Ellen looked scared. "My grandmother," she said faintly. "Isn't that right? Aren't there little rocks that come down and make you bleed and hurt you?"

"Right? It couldn't *be* more wrong." Janie stood over her. "There *aren't* any *rocks*. You got that? There *aren't* any rocks *at all!*"

"WOW!" said Harriet. "ROCKS!"

"Now, wait a minute," said Janie, holding up her hand like a lecturer, "let's get something straight here before you two get terrified."

They both looked up at her. Beth Ellen was frightened and confused. Harriet was angry and confused.

"Now, you must understand," said Janie, looking very earnest, "that the generation that Beth Ellen's

94

grandmother is was very Victorian. They never talked about things like this, and her grandmother thought that telling her this was better than telling her the truth."

"What's the truth?" asked Harriet avidly.

Beth Ellen didn't care about the truth. The rocks were bad enough to think about. What could the truth be?

"That just goes to show you," said Janie, looking like a stuffy teacher, "that people should learn to live with *fact!* It's *never* as bad as the fantasies they make up."

"Oh, Janie, get on with it," said Harriet. "What *is* the truth?"

"Ah, what a question," said Janie.

"JANIE!" said Harriet in disgust. Janie could be very corny and exasperating when she turned philosophical.

"Okay, okay," said Janie as though they were too dumb to appreciate her, "it's very simple. I'll explain it." She sat down as though it would take a long time.

"Now, you know the baby grows inside a woman, in her womb, in the uterus?"

They nodded.

"Well. What do you think it lives on when it's growing?"

They both looked blank.

95

"The *lining*, dopes!" she yelled at them.

They blinked.

"So, it's very simple. If you *have* a baby started in there, the baby lives on the lining; but if you *don't* have a baby, like *we* don't, then the body very sensibly disposes of the lining that it's made for the baby. It just comes out."

"Falls right out of you?" screamed Harriet.

Oh, thought Beth Ellen, why me?

"No, no, no. You always exaggeratè, Harriet. You would make a terrible scientist. You *must* be *precise*. It doesn't fall out like you say; it comes out a tiny bit at a time over a period of from, well, say four to six days, depending on the woman. It's very little at a time, and it doesn't hurt or anything. You just feel tired."

"*I* hurt," said Beth Ellen.

"Well . . ." said Janie, "sometimes there's a little pain, but it really isn't much. I just, frankly, don't care for it," she said as though she'd been asked if she liked a certain book.

"Well," said Harriet.

"Another thing I don't like is people making up these silly stories about it, like those rocks. Why can't people just take life as it *is?*"

Beth Ellen thought of her grandmother taking life as it is. She couldn't imagine her grandmother talking to her about babies, linings, Fallopian tubes, and so

96

forth. She felt a little sorry for her grandmother. She supposed that she had been trying to make it nicer for her, but it had been wrong because the rock story had scared her.

"The thing *is*," said Harriet, "does your grandmother really *believe* there are rocks? Maybe we should tell *her*."

"Of course she doesn't," said Beth Ellen, "and you won't tell her anything."

"That's silly," said Janie to Harriet. "You don't take into account how different each generation is."

"Well!" said Harriet, considerably miffed. "Instead of just lying there talking, why don't you make a cure?"

"I'm *going* to cure this one way or the other if it's the last thing I do." Janie looked determinedly out the window as though there were a cure sitting in the backyard.

"I just can't wait to not do this," said Harriet.

"Well," said Janie, "you might as well, since everyone else is. You'd feel pretty silly if you didn't. Besides, you get to skip gym when you have it."

"*Yeah?*" said Harriet and Beth Ellen in unison. They both hated gym.

"Yeah," said Janie with one of her fierce smiles.

"Well!" said Harriet.

That, thought Beth Ellen, is a decided advantage.

CHAPTER 10

They were having a discussion about where to go.

"Let's go back and see Mama Jenkins. She said come back one day before they work and get lemonade, remember?" said Harriet, looking at Beth Ellen.

That seems a thousand years ago, thought Beth Ellen, but all she said was, "Let's go to the hotel."

"'Let's go to the hotel, let's go to the hotel'—that's all you ever say," said Harriet.

"What hotel?" asked Janie. "Anyway, I thought people went to the beach out here. Isn't that what you come out here for?"

Harriet looked at Janie. Beth Ellen knew what was going through Harriet's mind: Janie was a *guest* and whatever she wanted they would have to do. She watched Harriet and her inner struggle.

"Yes. Let's go to the beach," said Harriet in a limp but friendly way.

"I couldn't care less," said Janie. "The sun gives you skin cancer anyway."

"Why don't we do all three?" said Harriet as though a light bulb had gone on in her head.

"Smashing," said Janie.

Beth Ellen felt a secret smile that she wouldn't let crawl out onto her face. She would see Bunny. Somehow her feelings about seeing Bunny had diminished in the light of her mother's intended visit and the discovery of her own maturity. Now the thought of Bunny came back as a warm childhood pleasure, as though he were a real bunny and she were starting out to find colored eggs on an Easter morning.

Janie and Harriet already had on their bathing suits, having gotten up in the morning and put them on immediately, so they pulled on some shorts while Beth Ellen waited.

"I refuse to wear this," said Janie loudly. They looked at her and she appeared to be talking to a shirt—a large, flowered shirt. "My mother put that in the bag, I know it. I've never seen it before in my life."

"I wish I'd never seen it," said Harriet rudely.

"Perhaps I could bury it somewhere," said Janie.

99

"I'll take it home to the cook," said Beth Ellen. "She has a lot of children and grandchildren."

"Excellent," said Janie and threw it to her. Beth Ellen folded it neatly and planned to put it in her bike basket. When they were all ready, they went downstairs.

Mrs. Welsch was sunbathing on the deck. "Your lunches are on the kitchen table," she called to Harriet. "I gave Janie something different, but if she wants tomato she can have some of yours."

"Thank you, no," said Janie. "I am not as mesmerized by tomatoes as your daughter seems to be."

Mrs. Welsch laughed. "I'm glad to hear it. I was beginning to think it was a disease she got at school."

They grabbed the paper bags and ran across the deck to jump on their bikes.

"Don't be too late," said Mrs. Welsch. "Your daddy's in Montauk buying lobsters. We're going to have a clambake tonight."

Harriet and Janie gave a great shout, "Hooray!" Beth Ellen looked uncertainly at the basket on her bike.

"Do you think you could come too, Beth Ellen?" asked Mrs. Welsch. Beth Ellen nodded.

"I tell you what. I'll call your grandmother while you're gone. I'm sure she won't mind." Mrs. Welsch had a nice smile. Beth Ellen smiled back, a big smile. How nice it would be not to have to think about

Zeeney for one night.

They waved to Mrs. Welsch and pushed off down the driveway.

"Where first?" asked Harriet without turning around.

"What's this hotel?" asked Janie.

"Okay, the hotel first," said Harriet, not hearing correctly.

Grateful that she hadn't had to ask again to go there, Beth Ellen pumped her bike with great energy and soon they were all flying along as happy as birds. The road was pleasantly flat and there were no frightening highways or railroad tracks to cross.

Harriet rode ahead a little. Beth Ellen and Janie, feeling the heat of the sun, rode slowly a little behind. Harriet was having doubts about spying in a crowd. She had never done it before. It didn't seem right at all. It was much easier to catch three people than one. She circled her bike around to come back to tell them this.

" . . . so then," Janie was saying as Harriet pulled alongside them, "the lining builds up again."

"Oh, for God's sake," said Harriet, "can't you both ever talk about anything else?"

She was so emphatic that they simply shut up and looked at her.

"Well," said Janie and smiled a superior little smile, "that's because you haven't—"

Harriet knew so completely what she was going to say and felt so profoundly irritated that she banged right over her, shouting, "Listen, you two, I may be undeveloped but I know a lot about spying and I never in my whole life ever heard of three people going spying."

They looked at her as well as they could, considering they were all flying along.

"So?" said Janie.

"Well, you have now," said Beth Ellen.

Harriet stared at Beth Ellen. It was totally unlike Beth Ellen to say anything sharp.

"That's telling 'em, Mouse," said Janie and laughed.

"Well," said Harriet, "if you get caught because you're inexperienced, don't blame me. And don't even say you know me. Nobody knows anybody if we get caught."

"We're just three strange girls who wandered into a hotel, is that it?" asked Janie, then added: "A likely story. What kind of fool would believe that?"

"BUNNY!" shouted Harriet and almost fell off the bike at her own wit.

Beth Ellen fumed but said nothing. Bunny wasn't a fool. He was a sweet man who played the piano. She thought of his sweet plump face as he sang and played.

Harriet, feeling much better, zoomed on ahead.

"Who's Bunny?" asked Janie.

"The piano player at the hotel," said Beth Ellen primly and rode faster.

Janie kept up and soon they were at the hotel. They put their bikes against the high hedge and Janie, not knowing any better, started to walk up the front path. Harriet grabbed her shirt and frantically pulled her back. "Listen here," she hissed, "you want to get us all killed? Now you follow me because I know what I'm doing."

Then they heard it. Beth Ellen stood entranced. It was the piano in the bar. Bunny was rehearsing a new song. Beth Ellen had to be pulled out of her trance by Harriet, who whispered loudly in her ear, "The best way into the bar at this time of day is through the front door. No one is there, and we can't go through the kitchen because the chef is there."

She lined them up like recruits. "The best way to go unnoticed is to just walk in without looking suspicious." She marched them through the yard and in the front door. The bar was to the right, the dining room to the left. Harriet pulled them into the dining room, which was empty. The long white cloths seemed to stretch for miles.

"The best thing to do," she whispered, "is to go in the back door of the bar so we come out behind the bar. Then we can see what Bunny's up to by peeking over, and he won't see us. Follow me." She led them

103

through the dining room to a back door which led into the hall and was directly across from the back door of the bar. They tiptoed across the hall and then, following Harriet's example, they bent low as they entered the bar. They were nose to nose with thousands of bottles and it all smelled rather bad. Harriet pointed them each to a different position and they took it. Ever so slowly Harriet peeked over the bar, then ducked down.

Well, she thought, this is really boring. There's just Bunny playing the piano. I'll let Beth Ellen get a good look at him and then we'll get out of here.

Just at that moment the phone, which was sitting on top of the bar, rang.

Bunny didn't stop playing. Someone will come in, thought Harriet, and being the good spy she was, took cover. The only problem with this was that the only place to hide was the beer cooler. She made a dive for it, got the top off and herself inside. She made a great noise on top of the beer bottles and her sneakers got sloshed, but it couldn't be helped. She pulled the top over her, leaving herself room to breathe, and wondered what the other two had done. Bunny stopped playing and answered the phone. "AGATHA, darling," he shouted. He always seemed to shout. "Yes, darling girl, I just this minute got back from Mass. I was just working out a little something here . . . working out, yes."

Agatha, thought Harriet; what sounds familiar about that? She wondered feverishly what Beth Ellen and Janie were doing.

Beth Ellen, even though dying for a look at Bunny, had thrown herself prone with terror onto the bar floor. Janie, her scientific curiosity having gotten the better of her, had simply stood up and looked at Bunny. His back was to her and he was too engrossed in his conversation to notice her, so she had looked a little and kneeled down again.

"Well, yes, love, yes . . . don't worry about ole Bunny, love, I'll take care of it. I'll just tell them that Mrs. Plumber told me to charge it."

Mrs. Plumber! Harriet almost stood up and yelled. He was talking to *Agatha Plumber*. Harriet couldn't believe her ears. Agatha Plumber was one of the very special people that Harriet had spied on all last winter. She was a flighty, aging socialite who was forever trying to find something to do that would interest her.

"Well, dear, I *do* think you should attend to some things here once in a while. . . . Yes, I know. . . . But we must remember that there's no manager. . . . Well, I know he disappeared. . . . But I've run clubs all over the world, Agatha, in Capri, in Rome, Paris, New York and—I do what I *can* here, but, Agatha, you're the OWNER!" Bunny's rasping frog voice was getting huskier with each yell.

Harriet sat stunned on the ice. Agatha Plumber owned this place?

"Darling, my wife and I ran a club like an oiled machine. . . . I don't care. . . . Then fire me. . . . I don't care. . . . You run this place like a pushcart!" He slammed the phone down and stomped to the piano. Great, billowing music filled the room as soon as he sat down. He played ferociously. He played so loud the floor boards shook.

Harriet stole from the cooler under cover of the noise. She beckoned to Janie, kneeling calmly, and to Beth Ellen, who looked up from the floor. They crept out after her.

Harriet ran like a wet bird down the hall, her sneakers sloshing. The other two ran over her wet footprints and then they were all outside.

"Thank heavens," said Harriet; "my ankles were frozen." As they were walking through the front yard they heard the phone in the bar ring again.

"Poor Bunny," said Beth Ellen. "He has to do everything."

Harriet looked at her. She started to make fun of her, then decided not to. "He probably does, with that Mrs. Plumber owning it," she said importantly.

"Who's she?" asked Janie.

"Oh, just some woman I know in New York," said Harriet airily.

They got on their bikes. "Does Bunny . . . is Bunny
. . . ?" Beth Ellen wanted desperately to know something about Bunny and Agatha but didn't know quite
how to say it.

"Gee," said Harriet, entranced by the idea, "I don't
know!"

Beth Ellen slumped inside. Maybe this Agatha
would marry Bunny and take him away.

"Come on," said Harriet. "Let's go to Mama Jenkins's." She pushed off on her bike and Janie and
Beth Ellen followed.

Even though the sun was hot now, they rode very
fast and were soon pulling into the driveway of the
Jenkins' house. A strange silence sat over the house.
They stopped in the back and looked at the empty
garage. The big pot was boiling away frantically, but
there was no one watching it. Most of the watermelons were gone, but there were still enough to feed
thousands of people.

"What is THAT?" asked Janie. She put her bike
down and went over and looked in the pot. "You'd
think it would be a fire hazard." She peered into the
bubbling mess.

Harriet was already up the back steps and trying
the back door. "It's locked," she said firmly. "They're
not here."

"It's toe medicine," said Beth Ellen to Janie.

"WHAT?" Janie was incredulous. "That's ridiculous. How can you make toe medicine out of watermelons?"

"Well, I don't know, but have you ever tried?" Harriet asked smartly.

"*Hmmph!*" said Janie.

"Come on," said Harriet. "They've gone somewhere." She got on her bike and rolled out of the driveway. Janie and Beth Ellen followed. "Let's go to the beach," Harriet yelled back at them.

Janie put on her big straw hat as though the cancer were going to get her before she got there, and they pushed on through the hot day.

CHAPTER 11

They were all sitting on the beach after a long swim. Janie was reading a chemistry journal and Beth Ellen was staring at the ocean. Harriet was working on her story about Bunny. She had decided that he had been brought up by a very old aunt because his own parents had disappeared. She planned, if she had not uncovered the note leaver by the end of the summer, to have Bunny turn out to be the culprit. To make this believable she had decided to have The Preacher turn out to be Bunny's long-lost father. She chewed her pencil and thought about this. Bunny didn't look a thing like The Preacher, that was the only drawback. Maybe it would be better to have Agatha turn out to be Bunny's mother, or just have Agatha marry Bunny and have the whole thing end in a lot of rice-throwing. It was a problem.

She chewed her pencil and looked around the beach. For a hot day it wasn't very crowded. She turned around and looked everywhere.

"Hey!" she said suddenly and pointed to the crest of the dune behind them.

Beth Ellen turned around and followed her gaze. Her eyes widened.

Janie looked up, irritated. "Can't we ever have any peace and quiet around here?"

"Nobody has said a word for an hour," Harriet snapped, never taking her eyes off the hill. Across the dune marched Mama Jenkins like a behemoth out for food. Norman and Jessie Mae tumbled after her. Magnolia was a dot, struggling.

"Listen, Beth Ellen," said Harriet, "this is our chance."

Beth Ellen looked at her in astonishment and Janie pulled her hat down farther over her eyes and buried her nose in her journal. They were used to Harriet's vagaries.

Harriet snatched her spy notebook and wrote:

WHEN THEY'RE IN SWIMMING, MAYBE I CAN SEARCH THEIR BELONGINGS AND WHOEVER HAS A RED CRAYON IS

THE NOTE LEAVER. MAYBE I COULD HAVE BUNNY SOLVE THIS IN THE STORY, HAVE HIM A DETECTIVE AND NOBODY KNOWS IT. BUT HOW CAN I HAVE HIM SOLVE IT WHEN I CAN'T EVEN SOLVE IT?

She watched them walking across the sand on the top of the dune. Norman was carrying all the towels and Jessie Mae a huge picnic basket. Mama Jenkins carried nothing and Magnolia struggled under the weight of a large green rubber dinosaur.

"HEY!" said Harriet and yelled all the way as she ran across the sand toward them. They finally heard her and Mama Jenkins stopped still as a rock. When she finally got underneath the dune so they could look down at her, Harriet yelled, "Why don't you come sit over here? It's cooler near the water."

Mama Jenkins looked down at her and laughed. "Hi," said Jessie Mae, and Norman scowled. Magnolia giggled.

"Let's go down there, Mama," said Jessie Mae.

Mama Jenkins chuckled and launched herself down the dune. She wore the same black dress she always seemed to wear, but this didn't stop her from descending in an avalanche of sand right to the bottom of the dune. She almost knocked Harriet over when she landed, but Harriet jumped away to avoid being hit by the rest of the Jenkinses, who came pellmell after their mother.

"Now, then, little chicken, where's a good spot?" asked Mama Jenkins.

"Over here, where we are," said Harriet, thinking as she did so, Janie will kill me.

She led them struggling through the sand over to Janie and Beth Ellen, who were watching her progress toward them with open mouths.

"Reckon it is cooler here," said Mama Jenkins, plopping down beside Janie, who gave her one agonized look and buried herself in her book again.

Norman, Jessie Mae, and Magnolia seemed to be all over the place at once, spreading towels and taking all their belongings out of the huge basket. Mama Jenkins didn't seem to care about towels but just sat right down in the sand.

"Jessie Mae, this is Janie. Janie, this is Mama Jenkins and Norman and Jessie Mae and Magnolia, and you know Beth Ellen." Harriet got it all out quickly because she was beginning to wonder what Janie would do.

"Hi, y'all," said Jessie Mae in a friendly fashion. Magnolia grabbed a drumstick from the picnic basket, and ate it. Norman ran into the ocean. Mama Jenkins nodded to them and fanned herself with a book. "Mighty hot, ain't it?"

"MAMA!" screamed Jessie Mae so loudly that they all jumped, "don't do that. That's the Good Book!"

Mama Jenkins looked with astonishment at the Bible she was fanning herself with. "Why, so it is. What's that doing here?" Jessie Mae snatched at it, but Mama Jenkins teased her by holding on to it. "Makes a mighty good fan, anyway," said Mama Jenkins and bellowed a laugh that made Janie sit straight up. Jessie Mae leapt at Mama Jenkins, but Mama Jenkins just calmly opened the Bible. "Look here," she said, reading, " 'Presented to Saint John's Sunday School in memory of Miss Eulalee Banks.' Who's this here Eulalee, Jessie Mae?"

Jessie Mae was grabbing at her Bible and now said in a whine, "You 'member, she's that little girl that burned up."

"Oh, yes, I remember now, that Harvey Banks's girl, struck too many matches, burned right up." And so saying she seemed to lose interest entirely and threw the book to Jessie Mae.

"MAMA!" Jessie Mae was horrified. "You shouldn't *ever* throw this book! This book is sacred!"

Harriet was watching everything wildly, looking back and forth at this tennis match.

"Ain't the book what's sacred, Jessie Mae," said Mama Jenkins in a bored way. "It's what's *in* the book that's sacred."

Jessie Mae stood stunned. Harriet, Beth Ellen, and even Janie looked at her to see what she would do next.

"I'm gonna take me a swim," said Mama Jenkins and heaved herself to her feet. "Come on, Magnolia, Mama'll take you for a swim." Without further ado she hoisted Magnolia onto her shoulders and marched toward the water.

"She has on a dress!" said Harriet, horrified.

"Mama don't ever wear a suit; she's too fat," said Jessie Mae, looking after Mama Jenkins in a defeated way.

They watched fascinated, as did everyone else on the beach, as Mama Jenkins walked straight to the water and straight into it. Magnolia clapped her hands with glee as Mama Jenkins walked solidly on and on.

"Well!" said Harriet, having no words for the sight. Jessie Mae sat down, smoothed her towel, and appeared to brood.

Harriet watched her through slit eyes, thinking. What kind of a pill would bring the Bible to the beach? It *must* be her leaving those notes. Who else would be crazy enough to? But how can I catch her?

Norman came back to the towels, dove into the picnic basket, and started eating everything he saw.

"Norman, ask the folks if they want some. Don't just gobble," said Jessie Mae, and when Norman said nothing, she looked at them all. "Would you like some fried chicken? There's plenty for everybody. Mama made enough for an army."

Harriet looked at Norman gobbling and thought, There's your army.

Janie reached out one skinny arm as though Jessie Mae might bite her. Jessie Mae gave her some chicken. Beth Ellen and Harriet said No.

Jessie Mae chewed distractedly on a chicken leg and watched Mama Jenkins in the water. She was sitting next to Harriet, so she spoke quietly to her. "I'm not sure but what Mama ought to wear a bathing suit up here. After all, we ain't in Mississippi anymore."

Norman sat down beside her. "Why?" he said with his mouth full. "It's cheaper this way."

"Money ain't everything, Norman," said Jessie Mae in a way that made Harriet wonder if this primness were being affected for her sake. "I'm just not sure it's God's way to wear a black dress in the water."

"God ain't everything either," snarled Norman and took another dive at the picnic basket.

Mama Jenkins was out of the water now, moving like a black armored car through knots of people whose heads jerked around in amazement. The black dress clung wetly to the strange lumps which made up her body, her brown hair was a straggle down her freckled face. But she was beaming and Magnolia was crowing with delight.

Beth Ellen was watching the whole scene with

enormous eyes. There was something about the good-natured, bearlike rough-and-tumble of the Jenkins family that made her feel nervous and somewhat frightened. They made her want to hide so they wouldn't suddenly notice her and jump on her or make her play some wild outgoing game. She looked at Janie, who was watching everyone stealthily from under her big hat. She knew that Janie wasn't afraid, because Janie wasn't afraid of anything. Certainly Harriet wasn't. Harriet was not unlike the Jenkinses, always leaping into everything and thinking later. Jessie Mae isn't so bad by herself, she thought; it's the others. She watched Norman eat. Incredible, she thought. I bet I don't eat that much in a week.

Jessie Mae was sitting beside her now and she looked at her in a friendly way. "Sure you don't want some? Mighty good."

"No, thank you," said Beth Ellen.

Harriet was leaning her head back to hear their conversation.

Norman and Mama Jenkins now began a shouting contest over everyone's heads. They seemed to be oblivious to other people.

"I'll tell you, boy," shouted Mama Jenkins, continuing some previous conversation, "long as you live with me you work, and that's the end of the whole thing."

"I'm not going to," shouted Norman.

117

"I suppose you want money," yelled Mama Jenkins, drying her face.

"That's right!" said Norman, taking a huge bite of pecan pie.

"Norman, you hush up." Jessie Mae looked like an angry pencil. "There's no reason we get paid. Mama wants to get paid too, and Mama's gonna make money and then we'll all make money."

"Listen here, you," yelled Norman right into Jessie Mae's face. "You don't know nothing. I been getting twenty-five cents a toilet down there to Bridgehampton where they done tore down that ole hotel. . . ." He reddened visibly as though he hadn't meant to spill this.

"Wh-a-at?" Mama Jenkins could hardly say it for laughing. Jessie Mae's mouth fell open. Even Janie got her fierce smile on and sat up to listen better.

"Tell me about this," said Mama Jenkins. She didn't seem angry. She seemed, on the contrary, to have a great deal of gentle interest.

"We-e-ll"—Norman dug his feet into the sand—"I saw where they was tearing down that old hotel over there on the highway and I saw all these toilets and I asked the man and he said I could have 'em for a nickle apiece. . . ."

Mama Jenkins gave a great whoop of laughter. "So you been making twenty cents profit on every one? How you been carting those toilets?"

118

Norman looked even redder. "Well, I used the cart and tied it onto Jéssie Mae's bicycle—"

"Is THAT why that bicycle has broken down five times? I oughta swat you right cross the head!" Mama Jenkins looked furious.

Jessie Mae gasped. "Why didn't you use your own bike, you mean thing?"

"Listen," said Norman earnestly, "I'm in business. That's my transportation. I got to have somehow to get around. You just use yours for pleasure. 'Sides, I didn't have money to get it fixed."

"Why, I think that's terrible," said Jessie Mae.

"I do too," said Harriet, and everyone stared at her as though they had forgotten she was there.

"You use your own bike," said Mama Jenkins shortly. Then she suddenly, inexplicably, smiled at Norman. "Well, I swan! You done take those toilets all the way the junkman, and you done made twenty cents profit on each one?"

Norman nodded proudly.

Mama Jenkins stomped across the towels and slapped him on the back in a rather man-to-man way. She and Norman looked at each other in a silly way for quite a long time. Then she leaned her head back and gave a great yell of delight. "Well," she said, smiling broadly, "you *my* son all right. Always trying to make a little. How *'bout* that? I think you make a better profit'n I do. I think *I* better go in the toilet business!" She slapped him again and he looked even sillier. Then she stomped across to the picnic basket and sang out, "Come on, you skinny things, my son and I'll teach you how to live!" and she began to hand out food whether anybody wanted it or not.

Beth Ellen looked at Jessie Mae and thought, I don't think I'll forget the look on her face as long as I live.

CHAPTER 12

At the end of the day, after they had waved good-bye to the Jenkinses, they took off for Harriet's house for the clambake. Soon they were rolling very fast down the hill that led to Harriet's cottage. It was at the foot of a hill and sat right on Mecox Bay. They zoomed down, hitting the rocks of the driveway, and Beth Ellen was sure she would fall on her face. She didn't.

They stopped and rolled their bikes. Janie stood looking a minute at the congregation of swan on the lake. In the late afternoon light they seemed to be engaged in some civic meeting.

"Look," said Janie. "See the big one in front? He's the leader. They all follow him."

"Mmmm," said Harriet, not caring a whit.

"Really?" said Beth Ellen, thinking the leader looked a bit like Harriet.

They went up on the deck. Mr. Welsch was lying in what looked like sound sleep in a deck chair, wearing only his trunks and holding a newspaper on his stomach. Mrs. Welsch was sitting on an air mattress, putting on suntan oil.

"What are you doing, Mother? There's no sun," said Harriet in such a loud voice she woke up her father.

"I put it on afterward. Hi, Janie. Hi, Beth Ellen; your grandmother said it was fine for you to stay. Hi, darling, come kiss me. Did you have a good day?" Mrs. Welsch smiled her pretty smile. Harriet leaned down and kissed a cheek that smelled of suntan oil and suddenly felt grateful. She was grateful that she wasn't Beth Ellen, with a strange new mother arriving, or Janie, with a sarcastic mother, or Jessie Mae, with whatever aberration of a mother Mama Jenkins was. She was so grateful that she ran and jumped straight on her father's stomach. He sat up with a great "Oooomph," and grabbing her, gave her a hug.

"Well, now," he said and yawned.

"Hey, Daddy, do we have to build the pit?" she said, bouncing.

"It's built. Why do you think I'm lying here like a dead man? Work all week, and what do I do on the weekend? Build pits!" He smiled at Janie and Beth Ellen, and they smiled back. They liked Mr. Welsch. "I know you, Janie. But who are you?" he said to Beth Ellen, who looked as though she might faint with embarrassment.

"This is Beth Ellen Hansen," said Mrs. Welsch.

"Are you—?" Mr. Welsch looked curiously at Beth Ellen. "You're not Zeeney Hansen's daughter?"

Beth Ellen nodded. I guess I am, she thought.

"Listen," said Mrs. Welsch a little hurriedly, "I think you all had better put on jeans. It's getting cooler and it'll get cold later. Harriet, give Beth Ellen a pair of yours. You have some, don't you, Janie?"

Harriet was not so easily dissuaded. "Zeeney is coming back!" she said to her father, much to the chagrin of Beth Ellen, who wanted the subject dropped immediately.

"Back from where?" said her father.

"I don't know from where. . . ." began Harriet.

"Europe," said Beth Ellen in a tiny little voice.

"That's a big place," said Janie, always irritated by imprecision.

"Athens," said Beth Ellen in a whisper.

"Come on, dear," said Mrs. Welsch to a grateful Beth Ellen, "let's find you some jeans." She led her through the door to the house. Janie followed. Harriet lingered, staring at her father, who was looking off at the bay.

"Yes, Harriet?" he said after a moment.

"Do you *know* this Zeeney?" asked Harriet in the quiet tone she used to try to make her parents talk.

"Well . . ." said Mr. Welsch, looking at the water as though he were in a trance.

"Well . . . WHAT?" Harriet asked loudly, trying to wake him up.

"I knew her," he said dreamily, "many . . . many years ago."

"What's she like?" she asked.

"Well . . ." said Mr. Welsch.

Harriet waited.

"Well . . ." he said again.

"Well, well—can't you say anything but 'well'? What is this 'well, well' all over the place?" Harriet forgot she was talking to her father.

He still looked at the water. "Well, she's . . . she's rather an extraordinary woman, that's all."

Mrs. Welsch came out on the deck as he was saying this last sentence. "Is that that skinny little Zeeney Hansen you used to play tennis with?" she asked Mr. Welsch.

"Yes," said Mr. Welsch. He sat up and seemed to come to.

"What's she *like*, Daddy?" Harriet insisted.

"A rather . . . *flighty* woman, I'd say, wouldn't you, dear?"

Mrs. Welsch looked at Mr. Welsch.

He nodded and smiled.

"Isn't it funny . . ." said Mrs. Welsch, and Harriet held her breath. "Isn't it funny how some days the swan are all over the bay and some days they disappear altogether?"

"Yes," said Mr. Welsch. "Where do they go?"

"Is that *all* you're going to say?" Harriet squeaked through her frustration.

"About what, dear?" said Mrs. Welsch blandly. "Oh, I must go start the butter melting!" She jumped up and went inside.

Harriet was in a snit. She sat down on the railing and glowered at the bay. Why was it, she thought, that the most interesting things in the world are always kept from children? Isn't there some way to force parents to tell the truth? They're always telling us to tell the truth and then they lie in their teeth.

"She's really not a very interesting woman, Harriet," said Mr. Welsch, who had been watching her. "She's a very silly woman, in fact. She never thinks about anything but clothes and men and money. People like that always bore me."

Harriet looked at her father with new admiration. Not only did he seem to read her thoughts, but he seemed to say sensible things. Was it a ruse? Was there really more to know about this woman?

"Do you know Wallace?" she asked.

"Who?"

"Her husband. Zeeney's husband."

"Oh. No." Mr. Welsch twisted as though he were uncomfortable.

"No. I don't know Wallace, but I imagine he's very like Bernard, or Mario, or Alfred, or the one before that."

"Oh," said Harriet, rather stunned and ill at ease now that someone was really talking to her like an adult. What did one say to this kind of thing? Her father looked sort of world-weary. Did one look world-weary back and toss over one's shoulder something like "Oh, yes, they're all of a kind"? She said nothing. She sat there, embarrassed, not knowing what to say.

"I wouldn't fill my head up with people like that," her father continued, "and there're a lot of them out here. But they aren't really interesting. They always do the same things and they really are boring."

Was this a put-on? Was this designed to turn her away from what was really very interesting indeed? Harriet debated. There must be some way to find out if he *really* thought they were fascinating and was lying, or if he *really* thought they were boring.

"How . . . uh, how did you know Zeeney?" This was dangerous and she knew it. It could clam him up completely. But it was worth the chance.

"Oh, years ago, out here, as a matter of fact, at the club. Used to play tennis with her. But she was rarely here, even then, off to Europe all the time. Studied in Europe, as I remember, whatever studying she did, which, I dare say, wasn't much." Her father had a dreamy way of saying this which Harriet couldn't decipher. He was always a little dreamy on weekends in the summer, but this could be a special dreaminess connected with Zeeney.

"Is she stupid?" asked Harriet.

"Well, no, she's . . ." he started and then turned and looked directly at Harriet, then said, "Yes. Yes, she's a stupid woman."

For some reason this made Harriet want to shut up about Zeeney. There was something powerful working in her father. He gave every indication of someone who didn't want to discuss something. He kept turning his head away for one thing. Harriet had long ago noticed that whenever people don't want to discuss something they always look away as though to drag your eyes with them onto another subject.

"Well," said Harriet, "it's a pretty day."

"Yes," said her father with obvious relief. "It's a great day for a clambake." He laughed and smiled directly into her eyes.

Mrs. Welsch came out then, followed by Janie in jeans and Beth Ellen in a pair of Harriet's jeans. "Oh, I can't wait!" said Mrs. Welsch. "When will it be ready? We have lobsters and clams and mussels and corn, and just *think* how it will taste."

127

"Hooray!" yelled Harriet, and Janie and Beth Ellen looked happy.

"Not much longer," said Mr. Welsch, getting up. "I'll go change and then we'll go look at the pit. Listen, Harriet, you kids better put those bikes away in the garage. You know what this salt air does to them." He went inside.

"Hey, Mother . . ." said Harriet.

"Don't say 'Hey' to your mother," said Mrs. Welsch, absently cleaning an ashtray.

"Well, anyway, can Beth Ellen spend the night?"

"Of course, darling," said Mrs. Welsch, smiling at Beth Ellen, who smiled at the floor. "I've already asked Mrs. Hansen and it's perfectly all right."

"Oh, good," said Harriet, watching Beth Ellen smile wildly at the ground.

"Come on," said Janie, "that ferric hydroxide is the devil to get off." She leapt off the deck.

"WHAT?" said Harriet, running after.

"Rust," said Janie pompously, "caused by an exposure to sodium chloride. Actually a combination of ferric oxide and ferric hydroxide. It tends to make pits in everything. Have you noticed the chrome on the cars out here?"

"I can't say that I have," said Harriet, rolling her bike furiously toward the garage.

Janie leaned hers against the inside wall and Beth Ellen did the same. Harriet was about to do the same, when suddenly she cried out. "LOOK!" She stood frozen, looking down into the basket of her bike. "It's HAPPENED!"

"What?" said Janie.

"What is it?" said Beth Ellen at the same moment.

They went over and looked in the basket. There was a piece of paper lying in the bottom.

"*I've* gotten a note!" said Harriet in rapture. She picked it up as though it were a jewel and read aloud:

HE THAT IS OF A PROUD HEART STIRRETH UP STRIFE BUT HE THAT PUTTETH HIS TRUST IN THE LORD SHALL BE MADE FAT

"What is *that?*" yelled Harriet. "What does it mean? Why would they send that to me?"

"It means you're stirring up trouble because you're so conceited," said Janie simply.

"AHA!" said Harriet. "You see they want to get me off the case. Well, they'll see! I'm not putting my trust in anybody but myself."

"That's just what it means," said Janie. "You're too proud. You're going to fall on your face."

"Too proud for *what?*" said Harriet, very agitated. "And besides that, look at this part, 'shall be made fat.' Who wants to be fat?"

"I think that means 'get rich,' " said Beth Ellen timidly.

"Oh, Beth Ellen, what do you know? Listen here, I bet you both haven't even thought that the only person who *could* have put this here today is Jessie Mae Jenkins!"

"That's ridiculous," said Janie. "*I* could have put it there, or Beth Ellen, or that Norman or their fat mother or even the little one."

"She can't even *write!*" said Harriet with disdain.

"Or your parents," said Janie. "You have a very sloppy mind. There are *many* variables in this."

"What would my *parents* do it for?" Harriet was turning very red in the face. "You're just silly!" she yelled at Janie.

"I may be silly but I certainly don't leap to conclusions the way you do," said Janie primly and walked out of the garage.

"WELL!" said Harriet loudly.

"Do you think," said Beth Ellen in a low voice, "that they want you to stop trying to find out who's leaving the notes?"

"Of *course!*" said Harriet. "That Janie hasn't been on this case as long as we have. She doesn't know a thing. This is a *warning!*"

Beth Ellen nodded seriously.

"Let's just not discuss it with Janie anymore. She

doesn't understand the whole thing. And tomorrow we'll really get down to business." She clapped Beth Ellen on the back as though she were a police chief.

They went back up on the deck. Harriet put the note carefully away in her pocket. Janie was standing on the deck. "Mum's the word," said Harriet, poking Beth Ellen.

"Of all the unmitigated clichés," said Janie.

Mum . . . mummy . . . mother, thought Beth Ellen.

"Where is everybody?" asked Harriet, ignoring Janie.

"They're out at the pit," said Janie.

Over near the end of the spit which curved into Mecox Bay they could see Mrs. Welsch waving at them as Mr. Welsch leaned over the pit.

"Let's go," said Harriet, and they all ran across the sand.

Mr. Welsch had taken the tarpaulin off, and with the aid of tongs, was heaping things into baskets as he got down through each layer. First there was corn, steamed in the husks. Harriet grabbed an ear, burned her fingers, and dropped it, screaming.

"Wait," said Mrs. Welsch, "just wait."

Then came a layer of steamed clams, then a layer of mussels, more corn, then the lobsters. They could hardly wait until it was all piled high on their plates.

131

There was a big pot of melted butter, which Mrs. Welsch divided into cups for each of them.

They all sat around on logs and rocks, dipping the lobster meat, the clams, the mussels, and covering their faces with butter and grins. Everything had a marvelous smooth, smoky taste.

"This is great!" said Janie, gnawing on her fourth ear of corn.

"Yeah!" said Harriet.

Even Beth Ellen ate a lot. They all stuffed themselves. Harriet lay back on the sand and pretended she was dead from overeating.

"That's the beauty of this kind of dinner," said Mrs. Welsch, "no dishes to wash." She threw her paper plate into the fire with abandon and watched it burn. They all threw their plates in and the fire roared up. It was getting darker and darker. They lay back, watching the fire glow and the dark come, all thinking their own thoughts.

After a while Mrs. Welsch stretched a little and said, "I think I'd like to walk out to the end of the spit. Anybody want to come?"

"I do," said Janie and jumped up. "Harriet says there's a swan skeleton out there!"

"There is," said Mrs. Welsch. "Here, I'll take the flashlight and show it to you."

"I'll go too," said Beth Ellen quietly and got up.

"Not *me,*" said Harriet. "I *ate* too much."

"You shall be made fat," said Janie and got a sneaker thrown at her for her trouble. She jumped away and laughed.

"I'll watch the fire," said Mr. Welsch.

They left and Harriet and her father watched the stars begin to come out one by one.

"Daddy?" Harriet said after a while.

"Yes?" said Mr. Welsch.

"Are you religious?"

"No," said Mr. Welsch, looking up at the sky. "That is, I don't follow any organized religion. That is not to say I am not a religious man. I don't know how I could look at those stars and not be a religious man. I just mean that I have made up my own set of ethics and don't take them from any organized religion."

"Do you pray?"

"No. No, I don't, Harriet. Why?" He was sitting on a log above her and he looked down at her very seriously, very sincerely.

"Because . . . I just wondered about very religious people." Harriet shifted around a bit. She wondered what it was she had wondered.

"What about them?"

"Well . . . I don't know. I just wondered. Do they really mean it?"

"Some of them. Some of them don't. Some of them just say a lot of words and they don't mean anything. It depends on the person. I do think, though, that we

133

should respect someone's religion whether we share it or not."

"What do you mean?"

"I mean, never laugh at anyone's religion, because whether you take it seriously or not, they do. And more than that, people who think enough to even *have* a religion should be respected at least for the thinking. Of course that's a trap too. Some people haven't thought at all and just follow other people and take on their religion without ever thinking at all. But you shouldn't even laugh at *them*, just pity them."

It was getting more confusing all the time. Her father always seemed to talk like this—very clearly in the beginning, and the longer it went on the more confusing it got.

"Well . . . I meant . . . suppose, for instance, someone thought about religion all the time?"

"It would depend what they're thinking."

"Well . . . I mean, like a fanatic."

"Frankly I don't cotton to fanatics of any description. They tend to think the end justifies the means, always. I've never seen a fanatic that didn't think that, and that's just stupid." Mr. Welsch appeared to be getting very heated. "How *can* it? When there never *are* any ends . . . everything goes on and on . . . so it remains that we are all *means*. . . . I just don't

135

understand why people don't see that. It's what's causing *all* the trouble today."

What *is* he talking about? thought Harriet. She decided to ignore him.

"Do you read the Bible?" she asked.

"Not now, but I have, certainly. It's a fascinating book. If you want to grow up to be a writer, there's no better book for you to read."

Harriet almost fell into the fire. "Really?"

"Absolutely. In my opinion, the poetry has never been equaled."

Recovering herself, Harriet tried to keep on the track. "Does Mother read the Bible?"

"Sometimes."

"She *does?*" Harriet was very surprised. Why would one read it when the other didn't? Did they fight about this? But she couldn't remember any real fights between her parents, only minor skirmishes which lasted a few minutes.

"Does she pray?" she asked.

"I don't know," said Mr. Welsch, looking rather fierce. "I don't consider that any of my business."

"Oh," said Harriet, considerably surprised at this. Didn't married people know everything about each other? If so, why not? She intended to know *everything* about the man she married. She thought she knew everything about Sport already, so if she married him she wouldn't have much to find out.

"You're full of questions tonight, aren't you?" said her father, smiling.

She wished he wouldn't do that. She didn't know what to say to things like that: Yes, I am full of questions? No, I am not, I am always full of questions? . . . Where another child would blush or mumble something, Harriet always commanded this situation by staring open-eyed into the eyes of the questioner. Few adults were able to withstand this. They turned away.

Mr. Welsch turned away. "Here they come," he said, looking out toward the spit, "and what in the world has Janie got?"

"It's that old swan corpse," said Harriet. "She likes things like that." They watched them walking toward the fire.

"Look!" said Janie triumphantly, sweeping the skeleton in an arc past Beth Ellen, who jumped away horrified. "Isn't it great?"

"I don't know, Janie," said Mrs. Welsch, laughing. "I don't want to see your mother's face when you get out of the car. It's no addition to a household."

"I know just what she'll do," said Janie with disgust, "run screaming into the house and call my father on the phone. Then they'll try to talk me out of it, but they won't be able to throw it out because neither my mother nor the maid will touch it." Janie looked lovingly at the long skeleton neck of the swan.

"Just look at that," she said, stroking the vertebrae.

"It's one of God's more beautiful creatures," said Mrs. Welsch. Mr. Welsch smiled at her.

"It doesn't look half bad, even dead," said Harriet.

CHAPTER 13

There were three mattresses on the upstairs sleeping balcony over the living room, so when there were too many children for Harriet's room, they slept up there. When they were all in bed, Harriet said, "Listen, I want to ask you something, both of you. Do you believe in God?"

Beth Ellen thought immediately of a dark night, long ago, when she had been only four years old. She had been with her grandmother and grandfather in the back of the long black car. A great storm raged and thundered around the car as it slid along the dark country roads. The rain beat against the windows. Mrs. Hansen had said something about God. Above the banging of the storm Beth Ellen had asked her grandmother a question. "Is God good?"

There had been a silence and then her grandmother had said, "Yes," very quietly.

"Why does he make storms that scare us, then?" Beth Ellen had asked promptly.

It had made her grandfather laugh. Beth Ellen had loved the moment because she liked to make him laugh. "You've got a very logical mind, little girl," he had said, and she had felt proud. The memory flew swiftly, taking only a second.

"I don't know," she answered Harriet. "I think I do."

"Janie?" asked Harriet.

"What?" said Janie loudly.

"What do you think of God?"

"Nonsense," said Janie promptly.

"What?"

"It's all a lot of nonsense. I don't believe a word of it. I told my mother that the other day and she fainted dead away."

Beth Ellen could almost feel Janie smiling fiercely in the dark. "A lot of people believe in it," she said timidly.

"Who?" said Janie. "Anyway," she continued, "that's their problem. A lot of people thought the world was flat too. So what? What do they know?"

"Well . . . how do you know?" said Harriet.

"I just know," said Janie emphatically. "There isn't any God and there never was one and that's that."

"Well . . . where did the idea come from, then?" Harriet persisted.

"Who knows where rotten ideas come from? Just throw them out, that's what I say," Janie snapped.

You couldn't help but admire Janie, thought Beth Ellen. She never seemed to be in doubt about anything.

"After all, you don't believe in Greek gods, do you? Well, *they* did, and then the idea got thrown out because it wasn't any good. I mean, after all, all those people supposed to be sitting on top of that mountain. Ridiculous!" Janie sounded furious. There was a small silence. "I guess," continued Janie, in a musing voice now, "that people made up God to make themselves feel better. After all, when you think about space, I mean *all that space* out there, it is pretty ghastly."

It sure was. Beth Ellen felt attacked by space like the slap of a hand. The thought was horrible. Space. Just empty space and her floating around in it.

Janie snored once briefly.

"Look at that," said Harriet loudly. "She knocked herself right out!"

Beth Ellen kept thinking about space. Was that what happened when the bomb dropped and the world was destroyed? Did it split in half like an orange and everyone just float around? Lonely, so lonely, it would be. And kind of embarrassing, humiliating for some reason, to be there all alone and no place to put your feet down and walk around. No one to talk to, just lonely thoughts flying around in your head.

"I don't know what's so bad about space," said Harriet. "I'd like to go to the moon. I'd rather go to Mars, actually. I can't wait to see what those other people look like."

"Suppose there aren't any?" said Beth Ellen, feeling lonelier than ever.

"Of course there are," said Harriet. "There's people on every planet, I'm convinced of it. They may look like shoe trees or something, but they're *there*."

Beth Ellen thought about people on other planets. Did they hurt? Did they feel things?

"What does it feel like when you believe in God?" asked Harriet into the darkness.

"I don't know," said Beth Ellen. I've never really thought about it, she said to herself.

"Oh, Beth Ellen, what a funny mouse you are," said Harriet with rather kind disgust. She turned over noisily in bed to indicate that the conversation was ended and she would soon be fast asleep.

Beth Ellen began to think about the beginning of the world, the beginning of time. Who started it all anyway? She let her mind creep back to the cave men. A cave. At the end of the cave, God. She was falling asleep. Right before she fell asleep she turned a corner in the long winding path of the cave and came to the end.

At the end there was a clay shelf. Spread on the shelf was a fur blanket and on the fur was a tiger, a huge tiger who said not a word but stared at her.

God?

Then who made the blanket?

CHAPTER 14

The phone rang the next morning just as they were finishing a big Sunday breakfast of pancakes and bacon. Mrs. Welsch answered it.

"Oh! How wonderful! Of course, yes, I'll send her *right* home!" She hung up the phone and looked at Beth Ellen. "They're *here!*" she said happily, her face a great smile.

Beth Ellen sank in her chair.

"Your mother and Wallace have just arrived and are dying to see you!" said Mrs. Welsch. "You better hurry along, darling."

"Hooray!" said Harriet and jumped up.

"Where are you going, Harriet?" asked Mrs. Welsch. "I think Beth Ellen would rather see her parents alone the first time."

144

Beth Ellen got up. I don't know if I want to see them at all, she thought.

"We'll just ride with her to her road," said Harriet, getting all her beach stuff ready and rushing out the door.

Janie shrugged and finished her breakfast. Beth Ellen thanked Mrs. Welsch and Mr. Welsch in a shy little voice, then walked to her bike as to the electric chair.

Harriet was already out the driveway. "Come on, Janie, we're going to the beach," she yelled back. Janie got up, got her things, and went to her bike.

When they were all three out in the road and away from the house, Harriet stopped her bike. Beth Ellen and Janie pulled alongside.

"You wouldn't mind, would you, Mouse, if we just got one little peek?" Harriet said in her most wheedling manner.

"I don't—" began Beth Ellen.

"We could just ride up the driveway on our bikes, and when they come to the door, we'd see them and then we'd ride right away."

"I don't think so. . . ." Beth Ellen hesitated.

"We could look in the window; they wouldn't even see us." Harriet was desperate.

"Maybe she doesn't want us to," said Janie. "They're *her* parents. You have to think of that."

"*Why?*" Harriet was beside herself. She hardly

knew what she was saying.

"Look, Beth Ellen," she continued, going so fast she stumbled over her words, "if we just rode up ever so quiet and looked in the window or hid in the bushes or ran around back or just waited in the road until they go out in the car, we could at least see them through the car window. That wouldn't hurt, would it? What would that hurt?"

"Harriet, why don't you stop?" said Janie, but she was bored with it, and putting her bike down, she sat in the road.

Beth Ellen looked at Janie as though her last hope had washed out to sea. In fact it had, because Harriet was relentless. "Beth Ellen, listen to this. If I don't *see* your parents, how am I going to know what they're like? Answer me that. How am I going to know?"

Beth Ellen thought it totally immaterial what Harriet knew or did not know, but she wasn't sure how to say this. She looked, therefore, at her foot.

"Harriet," said Janie, looking up, "you're a pain in the nose."

"Listen, Janie, you're my guest; you keep quiet!" Harriet was very moved by the prospect of seeing Beth Ellen's parents.

"I," said Janie, "am a scientist. *I* am able to take a *train*. I don't have to put up with *anything* from *anybody*."

Harriet's mouth fell open. Beth Ellen shifted her gaze from her foot to a scab on her knee. If only they could stand talking all day and she would never have to go home.

Janie's eyes were flashing. She and Harriet held an eye contest until Harriet broke.

"Well!" she said brilliantly. Janie looked away. "Janie?" said Harriet tentatively. She used the voice that she used when she asked her mother if she could go to the movies. Janie looked up ready to say No.

"Janie, it won't hurt anything just to see what they look like. We don't have to meet them. We don't have to say a word."

"It's *up* to *Beth Ellen*," said Janie with gritted teeth, and nothing could have been more definite.

They both looked at Beth Ellen. Harriet felt intensely frustrated. She wanted to shake Beth Ellen by her curly hair. No one ever seemed to understand how important it was to *see*, to just *see*, to see *everything*.

"All right," said Beth Ellen finally. It couldn't be any worse with them there, she thought.

Harriet whooped and they all got on their bikes again. As they rode into the Hansen's driveway they saw a long black limousine parked by the front door.

Harriet looked at the license plate. It was a rented car; she knew because her father had told her they

147

had special plates. "Hey!" she said. "Is that them?"

"How should I know?" said Beth Ellen. She was as white as a cloud. "I don't *know* them," she added.

"Should we go right in or around the back?" asked Harriet out of breath with anticipation.

Beth Ellen bit her lip, took a deep breath, then spoke so loudly she startled herself. "Let's just go right up to the front door. I live there, after all."

Harriet turned and looked at her with admiration. Janie looked a little worried. "We don't have to, Mouse," she said gently.

"We're going in," said Beth Ellen abruptly and pushed off. Harriet pushed off after her and Janie after her. It reminded Harriet of a troop movement in the movies.

They rolled down the driveway. Harriet wondered if they were being watched from the house.

The front door flew open and the most beautiful woman in the world appeared. She wore a white dress, and rushed through the door. She stopped, as though painting her own portrait, then flew across the lawn, little cries of "Darling, darling" escaping her lips.

The whole thing was such a shock to Beth Ellen that she fell right off her bike.

The woman in white ran toward her sprawled figure. Harriet braked to a stop, her mouth open. Janie had stopped immediately and now stood a short way back.

"Darling, my little darling, my cherub, my beauty, my sweet child, here, let Mummy help you," said the vision, bending to Beth Ellen.

Harriet looked her over carefully. To say that she was a beautiful woman would be an understatement. There was an extraordinary glow to her tan face; her thin body, like the body of a dancer, moved with amazing grace. Well, thought Harriet, I've never seen a mother look like *that*. I've never even seen any kind of woman look like that.

Beth Ellen lay there looking up through the spokes at what was supposed to be her mother. The beautiful white vision cooed at her, held out her arms, talked baby talk, and altogether frightened Beth Ellen out of her wits. She tried to pull her bicycle over her head like a blanket. This didn't look like anybody's mother she had ever seen. Not one of the mothers of the kids at school looked like this. What would Harriet and Janie think?

"Darling . . . come here to me, darling." She held out scented arms and half closed her large dark eyes. Oh, God, thought Beth Ellen, why couldn't she have been fat and wearing a flowered dress?

"Darling . . . ?" She made one more try at eliciting some response from Beth Ellen, then gave up, calling beautifully over her shoulder, "Wallace. . . . Wallace? Do come here, pet; she seems to be hurt."

Harriet and Janie stood straight and still, like first lieutenants to Beth Ellen's fallen captain. When Wallace appeared in the doorway, Harriet said "Wow" under her breath. "It's the Prince and the Princess," she whispered to Janie. Janie scowled.

But when Wallace moved he was disappointing. He didn't walk; he seemed to tiptoe. He didn't smile; he pinched his face in half like a glove doll. He's the strangest man I've ever seen, thought Harriet. He's like a man in a cuckoo clock, or a wooden soldier. Wind him up and he goes back to Europe.

He tipped over to The Mother. He peered down into the spokes. Beth Ellen shrank back.

"Hup, hup," he said, "here, here, girl. Give us a hand and we'll pull you out." Beth Ellen shrank more. "Come, girl, come on," he said.

Like calling a dog, thought Harriet.

He lifted the bicycle off of Beth Ellen, who looked then like a clam with no shell. Her mother lifted her to her feet and brushed off her shorts. Beth Ellen looked at her feet.

"Let me *look* at you," drawled The Mother, lifting Beth Ellen's face to hers. "Ah, yes, you're not bad at all, are you? You could do with a little fixing, but you've got definite possibilities."

"Harriet," Janie whispered from behind, "let's go."

She must have been overheard, for the next minute Wallace, The Mother, and Beth Ellen all turned startled eyes upon Harriet and Janie. They didn't say anything. They just looked.

"*Pssst*," said Janie.

Harriet felt strange. She wanted to watch. She also felt stupid just standing there. They obviously were not going to say the usual things that parents say, such as, "Are these your little friends?" or "Say goodbye to your friends, dear," or inanities like that. They just looked. It was impossible to do anything but turn around and ride off. She turned her bike.

Janie was already out of the driveway. Harriet hopped on and rode out to the road. When she got there, she turned and looked back. Beth Ellen was being led inside like a handcuffed prisoner.

Janie began to fuss as they rode along. "Why didn't you come on when I said to? They didn't want us there. Geez."

Harriet felt ruffled and somehow ashamed. She shrugged. "I just wanted to see what they look like."

"*I,*" said Janie, "don't understand how you can be so curious about *people*. I mean, *elements* or *why* certain things *do* certain things, I can understand— but *people*. People are just silly. Look at the mess they make of their lives. You can't ever *depend* on them."

"Well, I don't know anything about elements," said

151

Harriet weakly. She felt excluded, most of all, and rather hurt. She also felt lonely in anticipation because Janie was going back to the city tonight, riding in with Mr. Welsch because it was Sunday night, and Beth Ellen would no doubt be incarcerated for some time with her new parents.

"Of course," said Janie, "the person I really don't understand is Beth Ellen. She never seems to be curious about *anything*."

"Let's go to the beach," said Harriet. She was longing to begin a story about Beth Ellen's parents. She would make Wallace a swindler and have it turn out that Zeeney murder him in his bath.

CHAPTER 15

Beth Ellen was led inside. She was trembling. Her mother's hand felt thin and young, not like her grandmother's. Wallace opened the living room doors with a flourish and there sat her grandmother in her wheelchair. This was an occasion, because her grandmother rarely got up except for church on Sunday.

"*Well*, darling!" said Mrs. Hansen and smiled into Beth Ellen's eyes. She looked as though she were trying to gauge Beth Ellen's reaction.

Beth Ellen looked up at the familiar face and felt the lump of impending tears rush into her throat.

Mrs. Hansen didn't seem to notice. She looked at Zeeney. "Well . . . and what do you think of her?"

"Delightful," said Zeeney, dropping Beth Ellen's hand as though it were sweaty. "Do ring for something cool, dear; it's beastly hot," she said to her mother and collapsed wanly into the sofa.

"Of course," said Mrs. Hansen and reached out to give Beth Ellen a hug. "You know where it is, Beth Ellen. Run, pull the rope."

As Beth Ellen ran across the room to where the ornate bellpull was concealed behind the heavy drapes she heard Zeeney say, "And that's the first thing that must *go*. I can't imagine what possessed her father to name her Beth Ellen."

"I believe it was his mother's name, wasn't it?" said Mrs. Hansen, rolling her chair closer to the couch. Wallace seemed to half rise to help her, then sank back exhausted.

"That doesn't matter a whit now," said Zeeney. "It must be changed. It's perfectly terrible."

"You can't just change someone's name when they're twelve years old," said Mrs. Hansen in her close-to-anger voice. She looked at Beth Ellen, who was standing lost next to the bell rope. She motioned slightly and Beth Ellen came to her like a homeless puppy. Mrs. Hansen put an arm about her waist and Beth Ellen settled against her.

"We can, at *least*, call her Beth!" said Zeeney with what seemed like rage.

"Hup," said Wallace. Beth Ellen looked at him curiously. It seemed to be his noise, signifying only that he was in the room.

Harry entered with a tray containing bottles, ice, and soda. He put it down on the side table. Wallace leapt to his feet, suddenly alive.

"Hup, dear, what shall it be? Mrs. Hansen?"

"A martini in the veins," said Zeeney.

"Nothing for me," said Mrs. Hansen, looking at Wallace with a scrutinizing eye. "There must be a Coke there for Beth Ellen, isn't there?"

"Hup, yes, indeed," said Wallace.

Beth Ellen looked gratefully at her grandmother, who smiled and then hugged her.

"She likes that," Mrs. Hansen said kindly.

Beth Ellen looked over at Zeeney. Zeeney seemed to have forgotten her existence. She moved closer to her grandmother. I hope she never remembers, she thought.

"And then, of course, we'll take her to Elizabeth Arden's in Southampton. Thank you, darling," Zeeney said, taking the drink from Wallace. "I've heard that's the only oasis in this godforsaken place."

"Oh, I don't think that's at all true, Zeeney," said Mrs. Hansen. "There are some quite pleasant places about, little shops . . . even some nice places to eat, I've heard. I don't go out, of course, very often, and then just to the club, but—"

Beth Ellen was amazed to hear Zeeney talk right

155

through Mrs. Hansen. "Oh, yes, I did read something about one place . . . the Shark's Tooth Inn. That seemed to have *some* life. Who's playing there, do you know?"

Beth Ellen's eyes widened.

"No, I don't, dear, but I'm sure it's very easily checked. We could call if you like."

"BUNNY," said Beth Ellen loudly.

"What?" said all three adults. Beth Ellen lost her tongue.

"Oh, yes," said Mrs. Hansen, "that pleasant man we got for your birthday party. I believe you're right. Aren't you smart!"

"Bunny, did you say?" asked Zeeney. Beth Ellen nodded. "Bunny. Well, there's only one Bunny. It must be Bunny Maguire."

Beth Ellen nodded. She felt rather hysterical as the two worlds clashed.

"Well, that *is* delightful," said Zeeney. "Bunny Maguire. Old Bun-Bun. You remember, darling, that enchanting club in Capri, then later in Rome?"

Wallace looked up. He sat like an anteater, his long nose always partially in his glass, in an advanced state of somnambulism. "Yes," he said abruptly. "Hup, nice fellow. In Venice too, no?"

"Yes!" said Zeeney, seeming perfectly happy now. "Of course; I'd forgotten. Lovely Bunny. Why don't we take a run over there now and say hello?"

"Um, hup, smashing," said Wallace, finishing his drink in one gulp.

"But you've only just arrived," said Mrs. Hansen in some distress. "A lovely lunch is coming and I've ordered tea. Couldn't you go later?"

"Oh, Mother, we don't want tea," said Zeeney, getting up hurriedly in a graceful flinging of her long arms. "Come along, Wallace."

Beth Ellen looked at her grandmother's disappointed face. She loved it when her grandmother had tea every afternoon. When there were guests, there was a special tea with tiny sandwiches and little cakes. She couldn't imagine anyone not wanting it. Perhaps Zeeney didn't know how good it was.

"But Beth Ellen has only just seen you," said Mrs. Hansen.

"Oh!" said Zeeney, remembering Beth Ellen. "*That's* no problem. There's room in the car. She'll just pile along with us." Wallace had stood up and they were at the door now. "Come along," said Zeeney coldly.

"I don't think that's exactly the place for her—a bar? At noon?" said Mrs. Hansen.

"Ah!" said Zeeney and turned like a rattler. "She'd better get used to it. She's *my* daughter." She walked across the room and took Beth Ellen's hand. "She'll be safe with us. Come along, Beth. We'll go for a drive, and you'll get a Coke when we get there." She

157

spoke as though to a young child.

Mrs. Hansen wheeled her chair around as they got to the door. "Have the child back for her dinner, Zeeney," she said sharply, and when Beth Ellen looked back at her she could see the dark frown.

"Of course, Mother," said Zeeney and whirled Beth Ellen out the door.

Wallace had brought the small car around to the front and Zeeney climbed in, pushing Beth Ellen into the middle. She found herself straddling the gearshift of the ornate-looking sports car, long and black with no top and red upholstery.

"Hup," said Wallace, "hope the bloody thing works."

"Of course it will, darling," said Zeeney. "I *ordered* one that *works*. If it doesn't work, we'll send it right back and use Mother's Rolls."

It worked. It worked so well that they sped out the driveway at a hundred miles an hour. Beth Ellen watched the speedometer in horror as they careened and skidded along the country roads.

"MARVELOUS!" screamed Wallace.

"PERFECTION!" shouted Zeeney above the terrific roar of the engine.

I may be killed, thought Beth Ellen. She looked at each of their faces in turn and was amazed at the look of idiotic rapture shining there. Perhaps they are nuts, she thought as they narrowly missed a milk truck.

"Let's take her out on the highway," yelled Wallace.

"DO!" screamed Zeeney, and Beth Ellen wanted to hide her eyes. "No, no—here, darling, here's the inn."

As the words were leaving her mouth they were passing the entrance, but this did not deter Wallace, who simply executed a hair-raising U-turn, and they plunged through the gates onto the lawn.

"MARVELOUS, DARLING," yelled Zeeney.

Wallace cut the motor and leapt out of the car. "Cut the grass a bit for them, but it needed it," he said blithely.

"Get off the grass, get off the grass." A wavering voice came from the porch, and looking up, they saw Bunny's mother waving her cane and squeaking at them. "I'll call the police, the police. Now get that car off of there."

"Oh, God," said Zeeney disagreeably as she got out of the car. "Old ladies! What *does* the world need with them?"

She means my grandmother, thought Beth Ellen.

"Never mind, old mother," said Wallace as he walked right past her cane. "We'll be gone in a shot, hup." He disappeared inside.

The old woman raised her cane threateningly over

her head as Zeeney led Beth Ellen up the steps. "Not one step further," she yelled, "until you move that car!"

"Why, it's Mother Maguire, isn't it?" said Zeeney in an ever so cordial way.

The cane lowered and the old woman squinted at her. "You're Bunny's mother, aren't you?" said Zeeney, meanwhile getting swiftly past the cane and to the front door.

"Yes?" said Bunny's mother. "And Bunny wants you to move that car too."

"Yes, of course, of course he does," said Zeeney, pushing Beth Ellen through the door and into the bar.

"BUNNY!" screamed Zeeney as soon as she saw him. He was getting up from the piano, and he had on a beautiful orange blazer and white pants. Beth Ellen looked at him with longing.

"ZEENEY!" he screamed back, and coming over, he grabbed Zeeney in a bear hug. "Why, then, that's Wallace!" he said, turning around and looking at Wallace, who had already gotten a drink from the bartender and was being an anteater again. "WALLACE!" screamed Bunny, and running over, he slapped Wallace so hard on the back that Wallace choked.

"Hup!" said Wallace when he could breathe. "Bunny, old boy, *good* to see you."

160

Bunny was all over the place, grabbing chairs, ordering drinks. He suddenly saw Beth Ellen. "Why, this isn't . . . Why, this couldn't be . . . yours?" he asked Wallace.

"No," said Wallace shortly.

"*Yours,* then!" said Bunny, brilliantly pointing to Zeeney.

"Oh, don't be ridiculous, Bunny. I got her from the orphanage for the day. I heard you couldn't get in here without a child, like that lovely party the Hibbards gave on Mykonos. Remember?"

The three of them went into gales of laughter and whoops that lasted interminably, over that party. Beth Ellen, disowned, sat down.

She looked at Bunny. Was he like Zeeney and Wallace? He seemed more like them than like Mrs. Hansen, certainly, or like Mr. and Mrs. Welsch.

"But you *do* look familiar," he was saying, and looking up, Beth Ellen saw that he was smiling down at her.

"I think you must have played at her birthday party," said Zeeney, "although how you can remember out of all those grubby little faces, I can't imagine." Zeeney turned her back on Beth Ellen.

We weren't grubby, thought Beth Ellen. We were all dressed up. Even Harriet was clean.

"AH!" said Bunny. "Yes! That was it!" He put a finger on Beth Ellen's nose and pushed gently. "You'll be a beauty like your mother." He smiled, and walking over, he put his arm around Zeeney. "It's *so* good to see you. This summer is a crashing bore. Don't tell her I said so, but Agatha has no more idea of how to run a club than a jack rabbit."

"Not Agatha Plumber?" said Zeeney with a whooping laugh. "Is she *still* following you? I haven't seen her since Venice!"

"Oh, dear, yes," said Bunny. "Why, my dear, she owns all this."

"Wait till she sees Wallace! She'll faint dead away —mad about him, *mad!*"

Beth Ellen looked around. No one was looking at her. No one had offered her a Coke. She wondered if anyone would notice if she got up and went to sit on the porch. Their voices were giving her a headache. She saw Moo-Moo walk by in the hall, going toward the front porch. She decided to chance it.

She made it to the door without anyone seeing. She bent down and petted Moo-Moo, who looked up with cow eyes. She picked Moo-Moo up, and holding tight to her collar so she couldn't escape again, she took her out onto the porch.

She sat down, holding Moo-Moo tightly in her lap. She watched a car go by. Bunny's mother had disappeared. She and Moo-Moo sat all alone on the great wide porch. It was quiet.

She kissed the top of Moo-Moo's head. "We want

to escape," she said into Moo-Moo's ear. "We both want to escape."

After hours of sitting on the porch steps, which were growing colder, and listening to the whoops from inside, Beth Ellen noticed that someone had brought a chair, put it down next to the driveway by the corner of the hotel, and sat down. She could only see the back of a head. I hope that whoever it is doesn't come around here and talk to me, she thought.

A car drove in and a man and a woman got out. The head jumped up and Beth Ellen saw with amazement that it belonged to Norman.

"Right over there, park right over there," he growled at the man, who got back in his car and parked it at the far end of the lawn. When the man came back, he received a ticket from Norman, collected his wife, and went past Beth Ellen into the inn.

As Norman turned around he saw Beth Ellen sitting on the steps and scowled. Then he walked rather huffily to his chair and sat down like the chairman of the board.

Thank heavens, she thought, he doesn't want to talk. The whoops of laughter got closer to the door now, and suddenly Zeeney, Wallace, and Bunny were out on the porch.

As soon as he turned his head and saw Wallace,

Norman leapt from his chair, waddled over, and said loudly and importantly, "This car must be removed at once. The cars go over there." Then seeing Bunny behind Wallace, his mouth fell open.

"Never mind," said Bunny sharply, "these are friends of mine."

"What was that?" asked Wallace in wonder.

"It's the new car-park," said Bunny. "Can't say that I like the tone he takes."

"Frightfully clever of you to hire midgets," said Zeeney, sailing down the porch steps.

"Is he *big* enough to drive?" asked Wallace.

"Oh, he'll manage," said Bunny airily. "We have to do with what we can get. Agatha absolutely refuses to pay *anyone* a decent wage."

Beth Ellen looked over to see if Norman had heard this last remark. He had and was glowering. He's planning, she thought, to ask for more money.

They went down to get in the car and after much inane laughter and promises of dinner parties, sailing parties, picnics, and midnight swims, Bunny went back to the hotel and Wallace drove them through the gates at eighty miles an hour.

Even though it was only a blur at such a speed, Beth Ellen saw Jessie Mae standing behind a snow-ball bush. I must tell Harriet, she thought as they turned on one wheel. I wish I could just ride around like Harriet, only think about who leaves notes, and go home to a clambake every night. I wish I didn't have to ride down the Montauk Highway at a hundred miles an hour.

"HEAVENLY," screamed Zeeney.

"SMASHING," screamed Wallace.

CHAPTER 16

After dinner that same night Harriet sat alone with her mother. Janie and Mr. Welsch had left for the drive back to town. There was only a little time left before bed, and Mrs. Welsch was mending one of Harriet's shirts while Harriet fooled around with a jigsaw puzzle that lay out on the table. It was a picture of a painting by Utrillo. She felt nervous and irritated for some reason and the annoying little pieces just wouldn't fit into each other. She looked over at her mother.

"Mother, do you pray?" she asked suddenly.

Her mother looked up. Her eyes were very clear and brown. "Why do you ask?"

"Well . . . Daddy didn't know." Harriet said this hesitatingly, not knowing whether she should be saying it at all.

"He didn't?" Mrs. Welsch looked down at her mending. "No. I suppose he doesn't. Well, it's a very private thing."

Harriet felt she should say no more on that subject. She waited for a moment to see if her mother would say anything else.

Mrs. Welsch put down her mending. "We have discussed, however, *your* religious training." Harriet looked at her in surprise as she continued. "We decided that since neither one of us are churchgoing people, we wouldn't take you either. We decided we would let you make up your mind as you got older. Are you interested in going to church?"

"No," said Harriet quickly. Once she had been taken to church because a former nurse by the name of Ole Golly had said that she should at least see what it was like. It had made her itch.

"Well," said her mother, taking a breath, "what do you feel about God?"

"I don't know," said Harriet. "I don't know what to think."

Mrs. Welsch went back to her mending, then looked up again. "I happen to believe in God. I turn to him for solace and I also feel that I would be lost without him. But it is purely a personal matter. I think a person should think about it, not simply accept what is handed them, but think about it. You should draw your own conclusions. You'll know in time what you feel."

Harriet sat thinking about that. She found a piece of the puzzle that fitted and felt a resounding satisfaction. How silly, she thought, that that should make me feel so good; that a piece of cardboard cut out of another piece of cardboard and then fitted back in should make a person feel so good.

What my mother says sounds fairly sensible, she thought, but I wish I could ask her what she *feels*. What does it *feel* like to believe in God? What does Jessie Mae feel? Or The Preacher?

"Do fanatics froth at the mouth?" she asked her mother suddenly.

Her mother burst out laughing. "Whatever gave you that idea?"

"I heard it once," said Harriet. She had been very upset by this idea of frothing. It was one thing to think of The Preacher frothing at the mouth, rolling his eyes, and talking endlessly, but the idea of Jessie Mae doing this seemed ridiculous. Jessie Mae seemed altogether too cheerful to froth.

"It's an old idea," said Mrs. Welsch, "a very old-fashioned idea that fanatics are crazy and froth at the mouth. It's very hard to tell one fanatic from another these days. They look like very ordinary people until

168

you get to know them, and then you find out they're obsessed."

"Hhrumph," said Harriet loudly. This was very irritating. It meant that Janie was right. This fanatic could be anyone. She yawned.

"What about bed, darling?" asked her mother, folding up her mending. "You'll want to get up early for the beach." Mrs. Welsch went into the kitchen. "Want something before bed?" she called back.

Harriet thought hurriedly. What do I want? I don't want space. I don't know if I want there to be a God. Wouldn't He spy on me all the time and know everything I thought? Where is He, anyway?

"Darling?" Mrs. Welsch was at the kitchen door. Harriet looked up into her mother's warm smile. She felt a rush of love, a safety and a joy in the simple warm routine of bed, of being given food, of mother, of the house, of her own room, of herself.

"YES!" She laughed because it came out in a shout. "I want something. I want everything. I want corn flakes and sardines and lobsters and clams and shells with tomato sauce . . ." She made her mother laugh by running to the icebox, grabbing open the door, and shouting into the interior, ". . . and pickles and 'wettice' and orange juice and steak and potatoes and cake and ketchup and fourteen tomato sandwiches and everything, everything, everything!"

169

CHAPTER 17

The next morning Harriet got up, got dressed, ate breakfast, and jumped on her bike. She rushed to Beth Ellen's house without telephoning first. She felt sure that if she called, Beth Ellen wouldn't let her come over and she was determined to see more of Beth Ellen's parents.

She rode up the long driveway feeling that there were probably a million eyes looking at her from behind the dark windows which stood in rows across the front of the house. She parked her bike and went through the screened door which led to the back porch.

She looked through the back door into the kitchen

where Harry sat reading the paper. The cook was at the stove and the maid was in the pantry. Suppose they have left word that no one can see Beth Ellen? she thought. They may try and stop me. I'll have to make a dash for it.

She opened the screened door, shot through the kitchen, through the pantry, and out the pantry door in a split second. The maid screamed and Harry put down the paper with "What was that?" The cook turned around and said, "It felt like a wind. You'd better fix that screen door. I don't want flies in here this summer."

Harriet slammed up the front stairs and around the dark corner to Beth Ellen's door. She knocked.

"Yes?" came a timid little sound from inside.

"It's me," said Harriet in a stage whisper.

Beth Ellen opened the door quickly. "*Sshush*," she said and looked frightened, "they're asleep."

"I'm *quiet*," said Harriet gruffly. Beth Ellen closed the door. She sat down on the edge of the bed and looked at Harriet as though she'd forgotten who she was.

"Well," said Harriet, sitting on a chair, "what are they like? Do you like them? Your mother's pretty, don't you think? *I* think she's pretty. Janie and I talked about it. She's the prettiest mother we've ever seen. Do you like Wallace? Does he like you? Do you have fun with them?"

Beth Ellen just stared at her.

"BETH ELLEN!" yelled Harriet.

"I'm thinking," said Beth Ellen. "And anyway, I'm to be called Beth now."

"Why?"

"Because my mother says that Beth Ellen is tacky."

Harriet didn't know how to proceed with this information. She decided it had better be left alone. "Well, tell me. What happened yesterday? After they picked you up off the ground and took you inside, what happened?"

"We sat down, and then we got up and went to the Shark's Tooth."

"You're KIDDING!" Harriet was overjoyed. "Did you ask them to take you there?"

"No," said Beth Ellen, wondering how in the world Harriet would think of such a thing, "they wanted to go. They know Bunny."

"REALLY?" Harriet almost leapt across the room. "Well, tell me, tell me."

"There's nothing more to tell."

This was one of the more infuriating things about Beth Ellen. Harriet looked at her and wanted to strangle her. Just as a story got good she would invariably tell you there was nothing more to say. It's a good thing she *doesn't* want to be a writer, thought

172

Harriet, because all her books would get thrown across the room.

Patiently she said, "Something *must* have happened, *Beth*. You didn't go to the Shark's Tooth and then just go up in smoke!"

"We went there, and they went in the bar and saw Bunny and I sat on the porch."

"And?"

"And . . . Norman was there."

"WHAT?" Harriet stood up. "And you waited all this time to tell me?"

Beth Ellen looked at her.

"I just don't understand you. The most important part of the *whole* thing you wait till last to tell me."

"Shut up," said Beth Ellen.

"What?"

"Shut up."

"Well," said Harriet and moved to look out the window to give herself time to plot. She was too curious to allow herself to be insulted just yet. "You have to admit, it's like pulling teeth to get anything out of you." She turned back to look at Beth Ellen and suddenly noticed that Beth Ellen's eyes were red and swollen. She's been crying, she thought. Maybe they're hateful and she isn't telling me.

"What was Norman doing there?" she asked gently.

"He has a job parking cars," said Beth Ellen and seemed to be grateful that they were talking.

"I didn't know that," said Harriet, pacing the floor. *"Hmmmm.* Do you realize, if he's there all the time, maybe *he's* the one leaving the notes?"

"Oh," said Beth Ellen, "I'd forgotten about the notes."

"FORGOTTEN?" yelled Harriet, then remembered that she had better be on her good behavior. She turned and said casually, "Which one is their room?"

"Oh, no, you can't . . ." said Beth Ellen, looking terrified, "you can't do that."

"Oh, yes, I can," said Harriet and jumped to the door. She grabbed Beth Ellen's hand as she went by and said, "Don't *you* want to know what they're really like? They're *your* parents. You're the one oughta be pulling me down the hall. Come on. Don't you want to find out about them before it's too late?"

Beth Ellen's eyes got huge.

"Come on," said Harriet as to a child at the dentist's. "This won't take but a minute."

She pulled Beth Ellen up. Beth Ellen allowed herself to be pulled like someone hypnotized.

They crept down the hall. Beth Ellen finally pointed to a door. When they got to it, Harriet bent to the keyhole. She could see a beautiful room with sunlight flooding through the windows. Zeeney was

174

standing in front of an enormous closet choked with clothes. She wore a long white peignoir. Wallace was sitting at a small desk wearing white flannels and a white tennis sweater. He looks tweedy, thought Harriet, no matter what he's wearing. She let Beth Ellen get a glimpse, then pushed her away again.

Zeeney was talking. They could hear her very clearly. Even Beth Ellen leaned forward and listened eagerly.

"Darling? What, *what* should I wear tonight? Should I wear the wild red roses or this demure . . . Wallace, you aren't listening."

"Hup," said Wallace, who was jotting down something at the desk.

"The red one?" She looked at him. Her eyes widened as she looked at the back of his neck. "It all depends. . . . Darling, is it definite that Agatha will be there?"

"Hup."

"DARLING!"

Wallace jumped. He wore glasses which made him look as though he'd jumped from another century. "What? Hup, what?"

"Will Agatha be there?"

"*Hmmm.* Yes." He went back to his work.

"Are they going to the Shark's Tooth tonight?" asked Harriet in such a loud whisper that Beth Ellen shrank back in terror. She nodded. "Wow!" said Harriet. "Are you?" Beth Ellen nodded again.

"What's that rustling noise?" asked Zeeney.

"Mice, perhaps," muttered Wallace.

"What *are* you doing?" asked Zeeney in an angry way.

"*Hmmmm*, hup, working on my mountain, working out a deal about my mountain." Wallace began to whistle a strange discordant tune.

Zeeney stiffened. "You're *what?*"

"There's been an indication of some interest in my mountain. Do be a good sort, Zeen, and don't bother me. I'm working."

"On exactly what?"

"On a sale."

There was a moment of silence. Zeeney stood in an attitude that, had Wallace looked up, would have frozen him with terror.

"Do you *mean* the mountain that *I* gave you?"

"Hup."

"Wallace . . ." She frowned, then continued. "Wallace, do you think Agatha is trying to get you?"

"What? Oh, hup." He looked up with a wicked grin. "Yes, yes I'd say so." He went back to his papers.

"Someone wants to buy the mountain?"

"*Mmm.*"

"It wouldn't by any chance be Agatha, would it?"

"Hup."

177

"I do so hate that noise you make. It *is* Agatha?"

"Yes."

"Well, dear heart, I think I'll wear the yellow. Yellow always puts her out terribly because she can never wear it. Hideous next to that sallow skin of hers. There, that's decided . . . and I wouldn't be a bit surprised if she turns green—no! white! I shall wear *white!* I am ravishing in white! She will DIE!" She looked over at him, and knowing for sure that he heard not a word, she said, with no change of tone, "The way I'll look when I get back from Elizabeth Arden's! Jimmy is going to do my hair so high that I won't be able to get through the door. Dear Jimmy. He'll do the brat too, of course. *Her* hair is unspeakable."

She swirled around in a half turn which Wallace never noticed. "And you really needn't bother with what you're doing at all, you know, because I only gave you *half* that mountain. It's in the deed that one half can't be sold without the other. Your little Zeeney is smarter than you think. Agatha will have a fit. Although why she thinks you go with the mountain, I can't imagine. Breakfast, dear?"

"Hup."

Well, thought Harriet. He's just been had and doesn't even know it. Beth Ellen's eyes were the largest Harriet had ever seen them.

"Shall I ring for breakfast?" Zeeney came toward the door.

Harriet and Beth Ellen fled pell-mell down the hall. They fell, panting, into Beth Ellen's room. Harriet fell across the bed.

Beth Ellen seemed suddenly to want to change, because she rushed to the closet and began tearing out clothes. Shirt, shorts, sneakers, and with one jump she was into the bathroom and had slammed the door in Harriet's face.

Harriet lay on the bed thinking of her story about Zeeney and Wallace. Zeeney could murder Agatha, or run over Wallace with a potato picker. Why did Agatha think that getting the mountain would get him? Could you buy people? She suddenly wanted to go to the beach and work on her story. She pounded on the bathroom door.

"Beth Ellen?"

"What?" said Beth Ellen, turning off the water.

"Can you go to the beach?"

"No," came the answer, "I have to go to Elizabeth Arden's."

"*Rats*," said Harriet. "After, maybe?"

"No, I have to keep my hair clean for tonight," said Beth Ellen with a kind of desperation.

"Oh, for heaven's sake. I'm leaving," said Harriet and stomped through the door and down the steps, carrying with her the picture of Beth Ellen with her hair combed so high she couldn't get through a door.

"Lucky stiff," she muttered to herself. "Gets to go to the hotel and doesn't even care."

She shot through the kitchen again, just to amuse herself, and laughed when the maid jumped a foot in the air.

CHAPTER 18

That afternoon Harriet hurried back from the beach and began pleading with her mother.

"Please, oh, please, oh, please, Mother."

"Harriet, what's gotten into you? Why in the world do you want to go there? What put the Shark's Tooth into your head, anyway?"

"I TOLD you. Beth Ellen is going there with her parents for dinner. Why can't we go there? Why don't you and Daddy ever go there? It's a nice place and there's a good piano player. . . ." She gulped and hoped her mother wouldn't ask how she knew that.

"I just can't imagine what's so exciting about going there."

"Please, oh, please, oh, please, Mother. I'll do any-thing you say, anything, ANYTHING, for a month, for a year, for TWO YEARS I'LL DO ANYTHING YOU SAY!"

"Stop shouting, darling. You'll do anything I say anyway. Do you want to eat out tonight? Is that it? Are you bored with the cooking at home?"

"I want to eat *there!*"

"Darling, it isn't the kind of place one takes children."

"BETH ELLEN'S GOING AND SHE'S A CHILD!"

"But her parents . . . I just can't explain it. There are some places that you *can* take children, but it would just be better if you *didn't* take children. Now, we could go get a good lobster if you'd like that. We could drive to Montauk or to Amagansett. Would you like that?"

"MOTHER. That isn't the point." Harriet began again very patiently. "Beth Ellen is going there *to-night*. I don't see why we can't go there sometime, like *tonight*."

"Well, sometime we can maybe. I'll discuss it with your father on Friday. Maybe we can go when he's here."

"That's too LATE!" yelled Harriet in a frenzy. She ran past her mother's startled face, out onto the deck,

182

down to the bay, and plunked herself down in a miserable heap on some extremely wet sand.

At that very same moment Beth Ellen lay in the bathtub staring at her body. She and her mother had just gotten back from Elizabeth Arden's in time to bathe and dress before they went out to dinner.

She lay there with a blank mind. She arched her neck so that her hair wouldn't get wet in the back. Straight hair. She remembered that she now had straight hair. Zeeney had left instructions that Beth Ellen's hair be brushed out as hard as possible to make it straight. She had even discussed the possibility of straightening the hair by a new process, but Jimmy had advised against it.

She was reading her favorite book in the tub, having gotten it from its hiding place beneath the bed. She thumbed the pages carefully, if a little wetly.

I have straight hair. I am called Beth. She had heard Zeeney and Wallace discussing her that morning at breakfast as though she were a piece of toast. Zeeney had said, "I think her head is too little." Wallace had disagreed but said, "No. I don't think that, but she does have curious knees."

I have straight hair. I am called Beth. My head is too small and I have curious knees.

She wanted suddenly to duck her head under water

and ruin the whole thing. Her head would come up her own, great curling masses popping out with a will of their own. That's just what Harriet would do, she thought. She tried to imagine Harriet in Elizabeth Arden's and burst out laughing.

"Beth? Are you laughing in there?" It was Zeeney.

"Yes," said Beth Ellen softly and tried to hide the book behind the shower curtain even though she knew the door was locked.

"Stop playing in the tub. We are expected at six and I have to get you dressed." Zeeney's voice was cold, distracted, tight.

"I dress myself," said Beth Ellen.

"Oh, bother," said Zeeney and went out of the bedroom, slamming the door behind her.

Beth Ellen got out of the tub and dried herself. She hardly recognized herself in the mirror with her strange straight hair.

There was the noise of her grandmother's wheelchair. Then Mrs. Hansen's voice, very softly, through the door: "Do hurry, Beth Ellen dear. She gets into the most frightful temper."

Beth Ellen's first instinct was to grab her book and hide it in the linen closet. "Yes, grandmother," she said finally.

"And let her button your dress," said her grandmother in a strange, rather frightened-sounding voice. "She likes to fuss a bit over you, you know. And even though *we* know you can dress yourself, it will give her pleasure. You're to wear the white dress because she is wearing white, dear. Hurry now."

The wheelchair creaked away and Beth Ellen stood thinking. I would like to stick my head in the tub, run in naked, and splash water all over Zeeney's white dress. Why did she always wear white? Tonight she had decided to wear white because Agatha was wearing white. I will hate white, she thought, for as long as I live. I will never again wear a white dress.

After she was all dressed and Zeeney had buttoned her all wrong and her grandmother had rebuttoned her, she was led down to the sports car by Wallace. Zeeney was late because she had had to look in the mirror again. Wallace revved the motor loudly.

A bicycle crunched on the gravel. Beth Ellen looked up with astonishment to see Jessie Mae stopping next to her.

"Hello," said Beth Ellen suddenly, oddly glad to see her.

"Hi," said Jessie Mae. "I wondered if you and your friend could come to the house for dinner? Mama isn't here and I'm cooking." Jessie Mae's freckled face was alight with her plan and her small brown eyes were shining.

"I can't," said Beth Ellen, grateful that Wallace was so busy listening to the motor, he hadn't noticed. "I have to go to the Shark's Tooth Inn for dinner."

"Oh," said Jessie Mae, "I saw you there last night. I found out where you live from the garage man. Norman is working there now."

"I know," said Beth Ellen.

"He can't drive and they don't know it," said Jessie Mae in a very worried voice. "I went last night to watch out for him, but I can't go every night. I have Magnolia to watch."

"I'll watch him," said Beth Ellen, wondering how in the world she was going to do that. But she felt she had to say something because Jessie Mae looked so worried.

"Oh! Will you?" The freckled face relaxed and smiled warmly. "I guess I'll wait to ask your friend until you can come. Can you come tomorrow?"

"I don't know," said Beth Ellen, "I'll see." I don't plan to *live* at the Shark's Tooth, she thought.

"Come along, dear," said Zeeney loudly, sweeping past them, glaring at Jessie Mae, and leaving them swimming in her perfume.

Jessie Mae stared. "Is *that* your *mom?*" she said wildly.

"Yes," said Beth Ellen hurriedly and climbed in onto the gearshift. Zeeney slammed the door and glared at Jessie Mae again.

The car went out of the driveway so fast that Jessie Mae was completely covered in dust and even sprayed with bits of gravel.

"What in the world was *that?*" asked Zeeney, horrified. But she didn't really want an answer, so Beth
Ellen said nothing. A friend of mine, she thought to
herself and wished like mad to be going home with
Jessie Mae.

CHAPTER 19

"Now, remember, Harriet, I am going to have one drink and you are going to have one Coke and *that's it!* A promise is a promise, and you've promised me that you won't beg to stay for dinner. We'll just go in, listen to the piano for a while, and then go have a lobster."

"All right." Harriet was all smiles. She would have said all right to having her head chopped off. They were in the car driving to the Shark's Tooth Inn.

They rolled down the hill and the country lane had never looked so beautiful to Harriet. "Boy! Won't Beth Ellen be surprised!"

"I dare say," said Mrs. Welsch. "But is she going to be so happy with your beady little eyes watching every move she makes?"

"Oh, Mother." She laughed. Nothing could destroy her mood. The hotel was ahead of them. Harriet held her breath with excitement, then let it out with a great whoosh as they drove through the gates. "My God, there's Norman!" she shouted.

"What, what?" said her mother, narrowly missing the small fat boy who gestured them to a parking place.

"Nothing," Harriet said. "I just know that little boy."

"Well, even if you do, do you have to shout at the top of your lungs? And don't say 'My God.'"

Harriet didn't answer, because she was too busy watching Norman. He handed Mrs. Welsch a red ticket, then stuck the other half under the windshield wiper.

"Can you drive?" asked Harriet abruptly.

Norman turned his back on her and marched importantly back to his chair.

"Well, come on," said Mrs. Welsch, not seeing what had happened. "Let's go see what's so exciting."

They walked up on the porch. Harriet's face was bathed in the radiance of victory. She sailed through the door like the *Queen Mary* docking.

They walked into the hall, now brightly lit and festive, and on into the bar which was cool in the late afternoon light.

Bunny was just sitting down at the piano. He nodded a hello to Mrs. Welsch and then sat down to play.

Mrs. Welsch chose a table near the window. Harriet was all eyes. There was no one else in the bar except the bartender.

"Where is everybody?" she asked her mother.

"That's a good question," said Bunny right through his own music. He smiled at them. "It's early yet. They'll be along, be along, all be along soon enough."

"Sit down, darling," said her mother.

Harriet sat straight up, swiveling her neck around with delight. She saw Bunny look at Mrs. Welsch in an appreciative way, so she turned and looked at her mother too. Mrs. Welsch wore a lime-green summer dress, very straight and slim, which made her look very tan. My mother, thought Harriet, is pretty. She doesn't look like Zeeney, but she's pretty in another way. She doesn't look like she's going to bite your head off like Zeeney does. She looked down at her own dress which was yellow cotton with a yellow sweater over it that matched. I look all right too, she thought.

There was a loud crash from the back, followed by some hushed voices, and Bunny raised his eyes to the

190

ceiling. A waiter appeared. Mrs. Welsch said, "A vodka martini on the rocks and a Coke, please." He left.

Harriet kept swiveling her head around. So this is a bar, she thought. She had never been to a bar.

Bunny's mother came into the bar leaning on her cane. She said "Good evening" to Bunny. He looked away as though he'd been insulted. She hobbled into the bar and sat on a bar stool. Moo-Moo waddled in after her and went to lie at Bunny's feet.

Bunny began to sing. He sang like a frog. He had a small smile continually dancing at the corners of his mouth and his heavy-lidded eyes drooped in a sleepy, insinuating way. What can Beth Ellen think is so great? Harriet asked herself. He not only sounds like a frog, he looks like one.

"He plays well, doesn't he?" asked her mother.

Harriet was about to answer when she saw the most astonishing thing. She saw Jessie Mae standing in the middle of the dining room.

It was almost like seeing a ghost because she was only there a split second and then there was just a white tablecloth and the back of a chair. Harriet shook her head. Did I dream it? she thought. Of course not. What's she doing there?

In the next instant they heard a cry from outdoors. Harriet stood right up on the banquette and looked out the window. Jessie Mae was trying to drag Nor-

man away from a chair that he was holding onto.

"HARRIET!" Her mother was horrified and was almost pulling her arm off. "Sit down this instant. What do you think you're doing?"

Norman won, punching Jessie Mae in the eye.

"HARRIET!"

Harriet sat down.

"I've never seen such behavior. If you want to come to a place like this, you'll certainly have to behave better than that!"

Bunny appeared to be laughing at Harriet. He played very loudly. Harriet sat thinking. If Jessie Mae and Norman are here all the time, that puts a different light on those notes altogether.

"HOW SWEET!" and "How NICE it all looks" and "BUNNY!" came screams from the hall.

"AGATHA!" screamed Bunny, and stopping in the middle of a note, he leapt to his feet and zoomed around the piano to collide with the vision who stood, arms flailing, in the doorway.

"It *is* Mrs. Plumber!" said Harriet, delighted.

"How in the world do *you* know that?" asked her mother, now visibly aghast.

"Bunny, DARLING! Give Mums a kiss! Helll-OOOOOOooooo, everyone, your founder is here!" She flailed her way to the bar with Bunny bouncing behind like a fat foxhound.

In the middle of this their waiter arrived, and Harriet almost knocked her mother over trying to peer around his red jacket. She saw Mrs. Plumber give a resounding kiss to Bunny, one to Bunny's mother, and almost give one to the bartender before she remembered who he was.

"Harriet, do sit still, and don't stare so," said Mrs. Welsch.

"Bunny, DARLING! Just HOW is everything going?" shouted Mrs. Plumber, throwing an arm and just missing the bartender's nose.

"Splendid, love, splendid," said Bunny heartily. "Everything under control. Yes, yes, everything fine, oh, yes, oh, Lordy Day."

"And did you go to Mass, love?"

"Oh, yes, oh, dear, yes, every day, every day."

"And do you think silly little Agatha can run a club as well as your dear wife?" said Agatha sharply.

"Oh, dear, oh, yes, oh, Lordy Day, oh, Agatha, darling, I didn't mean to imply ..."

"Play us a tune, Bunny darling DO!" said Agatha, reverting to her screech and beginning to wave her arms around as though they were legs and were dancing.

Bunny scurried to the piano. The bartender ducked one of the arms as it came too close. Bunny began to play. Agatha began to sing in a quavering whinny consistently one note flat.

What an idiot woman, thought Harriet.

"Oh, dear," said Mrs. Welsch. She turned to Harriet. Her face had a bemused, rather wry smile. "Do you think you've almost had enough, darling?"

"Beth Ellen isn't here yet, Mother," said Harriet impatiently.

"But are you enjoying this?" asked her mother curiously as though *she* obviously wasn't.

"Oh, *yes!*" said Harriet, her eyes shining. Her mother laughed.

"Where ARE they?" said Agatha, loudly, peering at her wrist into a watch the size of an eyeball.

Harriet felt her mother stiffen and sit straighter. She looked and saw that her mother was looking at the door. She followed her look.

There was Zeeney, lounging against the door like an unwatered plant. She seemed to be holding up the trails of white which made up her dress.

"ZEENEY!" screamed Bunny.

"BUNNY!" screamed Zeeney.

They rushed at each other like two gladiators. As Bunny was about to collide, Zeeney put out a stiff arm and he fell against her hand as though he'd walked into a parking meter.

What are they doing? thought Harriet. They just saw each other yesterday. She looked at her mother out of the corner of her eye and was surprised to see her mother as engrossed as she was.

"DARLING!" Zeeney spat.

"SWEETIE!" sang Bunny and bobbed his head like a turtle trying to get to her face. Not being able to, he kissed the air all around her head.

"ZEENEY!" screamed Agatha and scuttled across the bar in the knock-kneed stagger which was her normal walk.

"AGATHA!" screamed Zeeney and they collided, each holding the other at arm's length.

Wallace appeared around the doorway holding the hand of a transformed Beth Ellen, stiff in a white dress, her face thinner-looking framed by the straight hair.

"Hup," said Wallace.

"WALLACE!" screamed Agatha and threw herself on his chest.

"WALLACE!" screamed Bunny and pumped Wallace's hand up and down.

"Hup," said Wallace.

"And what's this?" said Agatha, looking down at Beth Ellen.

Harriet got a wild smile on her face.

"BETH ELLEN!" she screamed and leapt across the room, arms outstretched. She clasped a horrified Beth Ellen in an embrace. Beth Ellen pushed her away and jumped back.

Foiled, Harriet stood in the middle of the group. Everyone looked down at her. She felt like a spilled drink.

"OO," said Agatha with obvious distaste, "it's Kiddy Night."

"HARRIET!" said Mrs. Welsch loudly. Everyone then looked over at *her*.

"Hi, Beth Ellen," said Harriet calmly, deciding to save the situation by acting as though nothing had happened.

"Hi," breathed Beth Ellen and shrank back.

"Harriet, come here," said Mrs. Welsch. Harriet turned reluctantly after waiting a minute to see if anyone would introduce her. No one did.

"Is this a little friend of yours?" asked Zeeney of Beth Ellen.

"ON TO THE BAR," said Agatha loudly, and grabbing Wallace, she pulled him forcibly to a bar stool.

Zeeney had evidently decided to play "mother." When Beth Ellen nodded, she said to Harriet, "What's your name, darling?"

"HARRIET M. WELSCH," said Harriet loudly.

"Harriet, come over here," said Mrs. Welsch again.

"Welsch?" Zeeney looked puzzled.

"Yes. WELSCH," Harriet said even more loudly. Beth Ellen looked as though she wanted to die.

"Welsch . . . are you Rodger Welsch's daughter?" Zeeney leaned forward.

"HARRIET!" said Mrs. Welsch in that certain brisk tone which Harriet knew could not be disobeyed. This time, however, she was too enthralled to do anything but stare up at Zeeney.

"Yes!" she said proudly.

"Well, *isn't* that the *most* enchanting thing! Rodger's *daughter* after *all* these years!" Zeeney held Harriet away and looked her over for any telltale marks her father might have left on her. "Well," she said doubtfully, "you don't look a *thing* like him. Are you *sure?*" she added vaguely. Beth Ellen looked mortified.

"Of COURSE I'm sure," yelled Harriet.

"Harriet!" Mrs. Welsch's voice was urgent.

"And *this*"—Zeeney was across the room in one white swoop—*"this* must be your *mother!"* She extended a hand to Mrs. Welsch. "I'm *delighted* to meet you. I've *always* wanted to see who Rodger married."

"Oh?" said Mrs. Welsch and for some reason looked at Harriet as though she wanted to tear her limb from limb.

Harriet looked at Beth Ellen. She saw her scoop up Moo-Moo and carry her out into the hall.

"I'm *so* sorry!" said Zeeney with a great show of white teeth, "I'm Zeeney Baines. I *was* Zeeney Hansen. Rodger and I used to play tennis together. We haven't seen each other since we were fifteen years old. He's never *mentioned* me?"

Mrs. Welsch looked calm. "I know your daughter

quite well," she said pleasantly, "and, of course, your mother."

"*Mmmm,*" said Zeeney, "naughty Rodger. Not even *mentioning* me. . . . What DAYS those were. . . . What CHILDREN we were. . . . Oh, the pity of it all. . . . *Les histoires d'enfance . . .*"

Harriet's eyes were bugging. She watched her mother's eyes narrow.

Zeeney seemed to pull herself together. "You weren't around then were you, dear? I don't seem to be able to place you. . . . Were you there . . . around the club, I mean?"

"Oh, yes," said Mrs. Welsch sweetly, "but I was much younger, of course."

"Of course," Zeeney hissed between her teeth and left the table. Over her shoulder, without even looking back, as she walked away she said, "*Terribly* nice to meet you. Give Rodger a BIG kiss," and she floated to the bar.

Harriet stood still. Mrs. Welsch looked after Zeeney with a smile of definite amusement.

As though forgetting Harriet were there, she said, "So *that's* Zeeney Hansen," and then she laughed, looked around and saw Harriet.

"What? What, what? What happened?" said Harriet without even sitting down. "What was *that?* What was that all about? What did she have to do with Daddy? Why does she talk like that? Why do you talk like that to her? What *is* it?"

"Sit down, Harriet," said Mrs. Welsch, and her voice was sharp. Harriet sat. Her eyes were very wide. She felt somehow shaken by this view into her father's past. Mrs. Welsch signaled the waiter for another drink.

"Do you want another Coke?" she asked Harriet gently.

"No," said Harriet.

"No, thank you."

"No, thank you," said Harriet and continued to stare at her mother.

Mrs. Welsch turned and looked at her. "Harriet," she said, and sighed just a little. "Zeeney Hansen and your father used to play tennis together when they were fifteen. Does that answer that incredible barrage of questions?"

"No," said Harriet. "RATS."

"Well," said her mother, "I don't know what you mean by 'rats,' but that's all there is to know about it."

"But the way she talked . . . and the way you talked . . . " Harriet felt terribly frustrated. She knew that she was right and that her mother just didn't want to tell her. This is one thing, she thought, that I really *hate* about adults. She knows I'm right and she just won't tell me. . . . She forgot everything—Beth Ellen, the notes, Jessie Mae, everything but this.

"Mother . . ." she began in a wheedling voice.

"That's it, Harriet. Now you mustn't dramatize everything." Mrs. Welsch looked over at Zeeney and her whooping friends in a distracted way.

"I'm not doing that!" Harriet yelled. "I saw the way she was and the way you were and I want to know everything!"

"Don't raise your voice," said her mother absently. Then in a totally different tone of voice, "Darling?"

"What?" said Harriet.

"Would you really like to stay here for dinner?"

Harriet felt like running in three directions. Dinner was suddenly a minor matter compared to this glimpse into her father's dark past. "Yes, I want to, but I also want to know this." She'd ventured out of bounds as she said this and she knew it.

"Well, drop it, or we won't do either," said her mother. The waiter arrived.

Harriet watched the red arms put her mother's drink down. I can ask my father, she thought. The world turned rose at this thought and she began to think about dinner. They were going to stay! She could watch them *all* at dinner! Her mother reserved a table. The waiter left.

"Could we get a table next to them?" asked Harriet.

"Darling . . ." her mother began, then broke into a

laugh. She looked at Harriet and laughed again, a friendly laugh as though she had just met Harriet and liked her.

"You can't have everything, darling"—and she smoothed Harriet's hair—"or will you ever know that?" And the smile her laugh turned into was sad and sweet. "We're *staying* for dinner," she reminded Harriet and then laughed again. Harriet laughed with her. Mrs. Welsch looked around the room. "Why don't you go ask Beth Ellen if she wants to sit with us in here and have a Coke before dinner. They don't seem to be paying much attention to her."

"Okay," said Harriet and went out to find Beth Ellen. Bunny struck a mad chord and began a wild thumping. More people came in. The bar buzzed. When Harriet finally found Beth Ellen, she was sitting on the porch steps deep in conversation with Jessie Mae.

CHAPTER 20

Harriet's eyes narrowed. She closed the screened door gently without going out onto the porch. Beth Ellen was talking earnestly to Jessie Mae. What is she talking about, thought Harriet, and why doesn't she talk to me like that? She hardly talks to me at all. Jessie Mae started talking now, quickly, as though she were fascinated by her subject. I have to hear what they're saying, thought Harriet.

She went through the hall of the hotel into the dining room. The dining room was empty. She ducked down under one of the windows which opened onto the porch. Partially covered by a long white tablecloth, she took up her post and overheard the following conversation.

"Norman and I, we know how hard it is and all, but we just determined we gonna have a church, a real church, a real nice church, and all the congregation gonna have long white robes, and we gonna immerse—"

"Immerse?" asked Beth Ellen.

"Sure, the baptism. We gonna have total immersion in the river. That's the best way, the only way."

Harriet had a vision of white robes wading into the East River at Eighty-sixth Street.

"We gonna have a pretty white church with real singing and real preaching and Norman says we're gonna make a barrel of money"—Jessie Mae was talking so fast she was spilling words—"and the people will come, and first we'll just have a tent, like the tabernacle, you know? And then we'll raise the money and build the church and, the Lord willing, be there the rest of our days!"

"How long've you wanted to do that?" murmured Beth Ellen.

"Oh, since we was little things. We *always* wanted to."

"Does Norman still want to?" asked Beth Ellen.

"Why, sure he does," said Jessie Mae. "Hey, Norman," she whispered around the corner of the porch.

"What?" Harriet heard Norman's gruff answer.

"Come here a minute," whispered Jessie Mae.

Norman evidently came shuffling over, because there was a noise of hedge and then of his voice much closer. "What is it? I got my work to do."

"I was just telling Beth Ellen here about our plans, about the church and all," said Jessie Mae in a chatty voice.

"Aw, Jessie Mae, I got WORK to do," said Norman, and he must have walked away then, because his voice got smaller at the end of the sentence.

"Oh, Norman," said Jessie Mae. "You know boys," she said in a flighty way. "They don't like to talk about anything."

There was silence from Beth Ellen. Naturally, thought Harriet, she has nothing to say again, just like with me. And then suddenly Beth Ellen began to talk.

"Well, do you think you should leave everything to God?"

"What you mean?"

"I mean, will God take care of everything?"

"Why, sure, honey, don't you know that?"

Harriet was so amazed that she stood up to get a look at Beth Ellen and zoinked her head against the table. Ouch, she said to herself as she rubbed her head and slowly took in the picture of Beth Ellen leaning eagerly forward toward Jessie Mae, who held one knee in both hands and rocked back and forth with a small smile on her face.

"The Bible," said Jessie Mae. "It's all in the Good Book."

Beth Ellen didn't say anything.

"Do you read the Good Book?" asked Jessie Mae.

"No," whispered Beth Ellen.

"Why, you *should*. It's the best reading and I read it all the time. It's the first thing I ever learned to read. Mama taught me to read that way. Norman used to read it all the time too, but now"—Jessie Mae looked over toward Norman and sighed a little—"he's taken to reading some mighty strange things, like the *Wall Street Journal* and things like that. I'm . . . well, I'm sorta worried, but . . . you know how boys are. By the way, that sure is a pretty mother you got."

"Thank you," said Beth Ellen politely. "She lives in Europe. . . . She just came back here. . . . I haven't seen her since I was very little. . . ."

Harriet listened in amazement as Beth Ellen started to confide in Jessie Mae. She had never heard Beth Ellen talk to anyone like that. She was becoming violently interested, when she heard Bunny and Agatha come into the dining room. She ducked under the table just in time.

"I *loved* my wife, Agatha—" Bunny began.

"Of *course*, dear boy, but she's *gone*, and *gone* is *gone* and when *gone* is *gone*, we must *behave* as though *gone* is *gone*. That's *all* there is to it! Now I'll give you one more year to get over her and then I'm

206

going to marry someone else—Wallace, perhaps. If you've not forgotten *everything* about her, I'm just going to marry someone else!"

"Agatha, this very morning I prayed for you . . . at Mass this very morning."

"And that's another thing. I'm sick to death of you going to Mass."

Beth Ellen's voice came through: ". . . and they're in there with their friends and I can't talk to any of them and I don't like this place and I'd rather not be here . . ."

Harriet couldn't decide which she wanted to hear most, and wished, as she had a thousand times before, that each ear would do separate duty.

". . . Agatha," Bunny whined, "you don't *own* me!"

"You WORK here," said Agatha imperiously.

"I must explain something to you, dear love, dear sweet Agatha . . . I will never marry you. I don't WANT to marry you, and I will continue to go to Mass all my life. That is my life; that's just the way I am."

"NONSENSE," said Agatha and swept from the room. From the hall her voice floated back, "You'll be over it all in a year, just wait and see."

Harriet peeked, watched Bunny follow Agatha, and then looked out at Beth Ellen, who was now silent.

"Gee, that's too bad. Well, I wouldn't do that if I

were you," Jessie Mae was saying.

Do what? thought Harriet. Do what? What did Beth Ellen say she was going to do? Why did I have to miss *that* part of the conversation? She wasted not a minute but ran right out of the dining room and onto the porch.

She clattered up to them and stood still in front of them. They turned to look at her as though she were a stranger. Harriet felt suddenly unnerved, shy, and as though she weren't wanted.

"Beth Ellen . . ." she began and just at that moment Mrs. Welsch came out on the porch and walked over to them.

"Harriet, I don't want you clattering through the halls. I'd like you and Beth Ellen to come in and sit down. Would you like to sit at our table, Beth Ellen?"

"Yes," said Beth Ellen promptly.

"I better be going on home anyway," said Jessie Mae, and getting up abruptly, she went to join Norman.

"Who was that?" asked Mrs. Welsch as she walked with them back into the bar.

"Nobody," said Harriet grumpily.

"A friend," said Beth Ellen.

Beth Ellen sat down and looked around the bar. She felt better sitting with Mrs. Welsch, safer and more comfortable.

I'm a child, she thought. I don't belong here; I'm

frightened. Bunny was playing very loudly now and Mrs. Welsch was watching him. Harriet was watching Zeeney and Wallace and Agatha at the bar. Wallace looked like a yo-yo being pulled between Agatha and Zeeney.

I want to go home. Where is my grandmother? I want to go home. Beth Ellen was overcome with longing—a longing so strong it made everything look sad, even the glasses on the table.

She could think of nothing but her grandmother's knees. When she had been very small, her grandmother had sat her on a tiny chair every morning to comb her hair. She had been at a level where all she saw was one big knee. The thought of that knee now made her have to bite her tongue so she wouldn't cry. What a dumb thing to think of, she thought. A knee.

She was going to cry. She got up, whispered that she was going to the ladies' room, and left the room. She felt extremely luckly that Harriet didn't follow her.

Bunny finally got up from the piano and said to Agatha, "I *must* eat now. You forget, dear, I expend an *enormous* amount of energy when I play."

"Oh, really," screeched Agatha, "not a whit more than *I* do, I can assure you. But if you must. Let's go, everyone." She grabbed Wallace and pulled him off

209

the bar stool. Bunny scampered after, leaving Zeeney to exit as gracefully as possible.

"NOW, Mother, NOW!" said Harriet, poking her mother fiercely in the ribs.

"Stop that, Harriet!" said her mother sharply; then, "All right, we might as well."

Harriet had to be restrained from running into the dining room. They were seated at a table only two tables away from the dinner party. Harriet was terribly pleased. Everyone was in full view and she hadn't missed a thing, because Agatha was still seating people.

"*I*," said Agatha, arms flailing, "shall sit *here* between Wallace and Bunny."

Zeeney glared and sat next to Wallace. Beth Ellen came into the dining room.

"Now *why* is there another chair? They're *so* stupid . . . oh"—Agatha suddenly stopped, then continued—"*oh . . .* that *child*. Well, down there; put her down there . . . away, *away*." She banished Beth Ellen with a wave and fell into her chair. Wallace and Bunny caught her. Beth Ellen looked timidly at Bunny and sat down.

"Harriet . . . HARRIET," said Mrs. Welsch, looking with irritation at Harriet, who was sitting on the edge of her chair leaning forward so dangerously that her nose was on the rim of the water glass. "What do you want first?"

"Shrimp cocktail," said Harriet without looking away from Beth Ellen.

"There," said Agatha. "That's over." She smiled winningly at Wallace and unfolded her napkin with an ugly snap.

A small piece of paper fell out of the napkin. "What's this?" she sang out. "Well, my *dear*, if it's a *party* favor, I haven't seen one since I was *six!*" She tried to read it but was too nearsighted. She was just saying "Wallace, be a dear and read this for me—" when there was an unearthly yell from the other end of the table.

Bunny was standing up at his seat, his face purple and upturned, his arms outstretched, the ugly gape of his mouth turning his face into the mask of tragedy. He stood one second in a caught silence of agony during which Harriet fell into her water glass. And then he yelled. His voice croaked and scratched its way out and flew in a burst at the ceiling. "I've HAD IT, AGATHA." He turned on her. "You silly fool with your silly jokes. You fat idiot. Here's your truth. I sit up NIGHTS praying you'll trip doing one of your veronicas into the bar. I spend DAYS praying your arms will break off at the elbow from flailing. You want the truth? I DESPISE YOU." He broke off, gasped for breath, and then screamed: "NATURALLY, I quit."

A piece of paper floated down from his hand onto

211

the table. Wallace, Zeeney, and Agatha stopped looking stunned and grabbed for it. Bunny's face broke in a paroxysm of rage, and so contorted that he seemed a cripple, he ran from the room.

"Sit up," said Mrs. Welsch, who had averted an accident by grabbing Harriet's teetering water glass.

"Sshush!" said Harriet, standing in her excitement.

Wallace read the paper aloud:

THE TRUTH SHALL MAKE YOU FREE

"*Oooo*," said Agatha, much impressed. She flung an arm, looked around uncertainly, then flung the other, thereby disposing of Bunny. With a great smile, she announced triumphantly, "THAT takes care of THAT!"

Zeeney smiled.

"Hup," said Wallace, looking under his napkin, "I think perhaps we all have notes."

Harriet looked at Beth Ellen. Beth Ellen looked petrified, her eyes as big as soup plates. "Hhrumph," said Harriet, sitting down and forgetting she was talking to her mother. "Wonder what she thinks of that Bunny now?"

"What, dear?" said her mother, a little absently because she too found it hard not to look at the center table.

"Mine, mine first," Agatha was saying, waving her paper in Wallace's face. He read it:

IF THOU WILT BE PERFECT GO SELL WHAT YOU HAVE AND GIVE IT TO THE POOR. THEN YOU'LL HAVE SOMETHING WHEN YOU GET TO HEAVEN

"*Oooooo,*" said Agatha with great joy, "isn't this *fun!* It's like some kind of nasty fortune cookie!"

"Oh, what's yours, darling?" Zeeney was getting rather excited about the whole thing. "I can't seem to find mine. And let's see if you have one, Beth." She grabbed at Beth Ellen's napkin and unfolded a paper.

Wallace read his:

YOU NEED MORE PULL TO GET A RICH MAN INTO HEAVEN THAN TO GET A CAMEL THROUGH THE EYE OF A NEEDLE

Zeeney laughed a most evil laugh. Wallace looked annoyed. "I don't think that's true at *all!*" said Agatha. "After all, who *has* any pull but the rich?"

"Let's see yours." Zeeney picked up Beth Ellen's and read:

AS IS THE MOTHER SO IS HER DAUGHTER

Zeeney crowed with joy: "I think that's *lovely!*"

Beth Ellen looked a little sick. She glanced over at Harriet. Harriet was staring at her. She could see Mrs. Welsch trying to get Harriet to eat a shrimp cocktail.

"Hup!" said Wallace. "Here's yours, Zeen, ole girl." And he read it:

IN SORROW THOU SHALT BRING FORTH CHILDREN

Zeeney grabbed her throat as though she were being choked. Wallace looked at her squinty-eyed.

"Now what does *that* have to do with *me?*" said Zeeney, looking straight into Wallace's eyes, arching her back and throwing one arm across the table.

Wallace looked more squinty-eyed.

Agatha gave a whoop of laughter.

"You see, it is a silly game," said Zeeney airily, "a ridiculous game. Whoever is doing it"—she looked at Agatha—"at least should have the sense to have them *apply.* . . . I mean, what possible point could there be if—"

"They *do* apply, Zeeney," said Wallace with a voice like a knife.

"Well, *mine* doesn't," said Zeeney and suddenly stood up, folded her napkin, and looked at Agatha. "I can't imagine what little joke you think you're hav-

214

ing, but I've a big fat piece of news for you—it isn't funny!" She threw her napkin at Agatha like a gauntlet and left the room.

"Why, whatever can she mean?" said Agatha, looking around in amazement. "Why in the world would she think *I* would do a thing like this?"

"Hup," said Wallace, his eyes narrowing so they almost disappeared.

"Well, never mind," said Agatha. "You and *I* can have a lovely little dinner together." She leaned toward Wallace, then saw Beth Ellen. She gave Beth Ellen a long, stony look. Beth Ellen began to slide off her chair. She looked terrified.

Harriet was beside herself. "BETH ELLEN," she shouted, "COME OVER HERE!"

Mrs. Welsch grabbed Harriet's arm. "We're going home," she said firmly, "and I think we'll take Beth Ellen with us."

She stood up and dragged Harriet over to the center table.

"How do you do. I am Mrs. Rodger Welsch," she said, extending her hand to Wallace. "I think that perhaps Beth Ellen could come and spend the night with my daughter, Harriet. They go to the same school and—"

Wallace interrupted her, relief flooding his face like a spring shower. "Delighted," he said, jumping up. "Yes, hup, marvelous idea—can't imagine where her mother is—smashing idea. Suppose her mother'll know where to find you and all that?"

"I'll call Mrs. Hansen the moment we get home," said Mrs. Welsch briskly, starting to leave.

"Delighted, thank you. Yes, hup, return the favor some day," said Wallace, bending forward as Agatha looked at him with rage.

"It will never come up," said Mrs. Welsch. And putting out a hand to Beth Ellen, she said, "Have you got a sweater, dear?"

Beth Ellen picked up her sweater and nodded to Mrs. Welsch, looking up at her with a face aglow with adoration.

"Then come along," said Mrs. Welsch and swept from the room like the Pied Piper.

When they were driving out of the gates Harriet started: "*Well! What* do you think of *that?* What in the world was that? Who was *in* there? I *saw* Jessie Mae go in—"

"We are not going to discuss it," said Mrs. Welsch, cutting her short. "It's been a very trying night for everyone, and I'm sure that Beth Ellen would be as glad as I would be never to hear it mentioned again."

Beth Ellen felt a wash of gratitude for Mrs. Welsch. She also felt on the verge of tears. She wanted to nuzzle her head against the sleeve of Mrs. Welsch's sweater. She also felt hungry.

Harriet sulked a little, but when no one paid any attention, she looked out of the window and thought her own dark thoughts for the rest of the way.

After Mrs. Welsch had called Mrs. Hansen, made some eggs, and fed them all, Beth Ellen and Harriet got ready for bed. Beth Ellen looked at herself in the mirror as she washed her face. Her mouth was a hard little line and her eyes looked small and rather purple. Something is happening to me, she thought.

She put on a pair of Harriet's pajamas and looked down at her feet sticking out of the bottoms. She went into Harriet's room.

Harriet looked at her as though she were going to say something; but she evidently changed her mind, because she just looked at Beth Ellen, then turned and got in bed.

Beth Ellen felt grateful again to Mrs. Welsch. She got into bed and Harriet turned off the light.

Harriet said, "Good night," softly, then turned over with a big flop.

Beth Ellen said, "Good night," and lying back, she stared up at the ceiling. The room was lighted by the full moon. A dreadful emptiness overtook her. I am as empty as the ceiling, she thought, and her heart began to beat faster. I am going to cry or I am going to explode, I don't know which. Sobs shook her.

A sweaty little hand came over and held hers. I like Harriet, she thought through her tears; she never

217

seems to have any feelings, but she does. She stopped crying. The sweaty little hand went away and there was a loud snore from Harriet.

I am tired of being this way. I am tired of crying. I can't cry anymore or something will happen to me. I am not going to cry anymore. I don't care what happens; I am not going to cry anymore. These thoughts went through Beth Ellen's head like machine gun bullets.

I will be different in the morning, she thought with a feeling close to contentment, and rolled over on her side into sleep.

CHAPTER 21

The next morning they were eating breakfast, when Harriet said, "I'll ride you home on my bike. Okay?"

"Okay," said Beth Ellen, then thought, I don't want to go home.

"And then can we go to the beach?" asked Harriet.

"Jessie Mae asked me to come see her," said Beth Ellen.

"Well!"

"No, I mean, both of us."

"That's *different*."

"She said she'd take us to see The Preacher. Do you want to?"

"SURE!" Harriet leaned forward. "I think it's Jessie Mae, don't you?"

"What?"

"Who's leaving the notes."

"*Ummmm.*" Beth Ellen had a mouthful of cereal.

"Well, do you?"

"I don't know. She seems nice when you talk to her."

"Hey," said Harriet. "What was it she told you you oughta stop doing?"

"What?" said Beth Ellen sharply. "Were you listening?"

"Yes."

"Well, it was private."

Harriet looked thoughtful. "Well," she said, "all she talks about is religion. You'd think she'd never heard of anything else."

"Why do you care so much who's leaving the notes?"

"*Because,*" said Harriet, exasperated, "I'm writing a story about someone leaving notes, and I'm making up it's Jessie Mae."

"Janie said it could be anybody."

"What does Janie know? She wouldn't recognize her own mother unless she saw her under a microscope."

"She knows a *lot,*" said Beth Ellen and was surprised at her own vehemence.

Harriet looked at her. "Listen, Mouse . . ." she began.

"Let's go now," said Beth Ellen quickly.

"Listen here, Mouse—"

"And don't call me MOUSE!" Beth Ellen was standing by the door to the deck and she screamed the last word.

Harriet looked totally shocked. Beth Ellen went out on the deck. Harriet shrugged, got up, and followed her out.

They got Harriet's bike, said good-bye to Mrs. Welsch, and pushed off down the road.

Beth Ellen was riding in the basket. As she rode along she felt oddly protected. Whatever one thinks of Harriet, she thought to herself, one always feels safe with her. Even her rudeness was better than the icy chill of polite parents. She thought what she had thought the other day, that being with Harriet made her feel that she could be a child for once. She felt happy feeling like a child. Most of the time she felt like a troll.

Harriet was humming a little tune, pumping away hard because of the extra weight.

Beth Ellen began to think of the night before. When I am married, she thought, I will make pancakes every night for dinner and we will never, *never* go out. She went off into a fantasy of herself, beautiful, in her own house, also beautiful, and Zeeney and Wallace all dead and buried. She got a picture in her mind of her husband looking just like Wallace and demanding that they go out to dinner. She refused. He hit her. She cut off his head and hid him in the basement.

"Look, there she is," said Harriet.

Beth Ellen shook away her dream and looked. There was Jessie Mae in the filling station again. They pulled in.

"Thanks very much," Jessie Mae was saying to the filling station man.

"Hi," said Harriet, running into the end of Jessie Mae's bike.

"Why, hi there," said Jessie Mae warmly.

"Hi," said Beth Ellen.

They all three stood there.

"Mighty hot, ain't it?" said Jessie Mae.

"Can we go to The Preacher's house?" asked Harriet bluntly.

"Sure," said Jessie Mae and looked around. "I was trying to find Norman but I guess it's impossible. He's disappeared."

"Probably out selling toilets," said Harriet and laughed.

Jessie Mae gave her head a little toss and turned to Beth Ellen. "Would you like to see my church?"

"CHURCH?" shouted Harriet. "We're not going to any church!"

"If you want to," said Beth Ellen politely.

"I didn't mean go into a church," said Jessie Mae to Harriet. "I meant come to *my* church, my church we *made*."

"What?" Harriet looked frantic. "What is all this?"

Jessie Mae climbed on her bike and started rolling. "Follow me and I'll show you," she called over her shoulder. Soon she was far down the road.

"Let's go," said Beth Ellen to an open-mouthed Harriet. Beth Ellen felt suddenly good.

"Okay," said Harriet dubiously, and the bike started moving. "But," she said slyly, "I thought you might want to go to the inn and see Bunny."

"Oh, Bunny," said Beth Ellen with disgust. "Who cares about Bunny?"

"Well! *That's* a change," Harriet panted as she attempted to follow Jessie Mae. "Now maybe we can spy on somebody interesting instead of hanging around there the rest of the summer. You mean you never want to go see him again?"

"I didn't say that." Beth Ellen was amazed at herself. The words had flown right out of her mouth as though she had absolutely no control over them. Was she tired of Bunny? He was like Wallace and Zeeney. Still, it hurt to give him up as though he were a toy and she had outgrown him. Maybe he wasn't so bad. Maybe Wallace and Zeeney weren't so bad either. Maybe she should give them another chance.

She determined to do that when she got home. Even though they were only paper dolls, it was hard to give them up too.

"You don't know what you want," Harriet was muttering.

Jessie Mae slowed down ahead of them. They were deep into the country now. When they stopped, they were on a small rise with woods on either side.

"Right up yonder is The Preacher's," said Jessie Mae, pointing to a little dirt road leading up a hill. She smiled sweetly. "But right over here's my church."

They looked after her pointing finger but saw only woods.

"Where?" said Harriet.

"Right over there," said Jessie Mae, grinning and pointing at the woods.

"There's nothing *over there*," said Harriet with exaggerated patience.

It occurred to Beth Ellen that perhaps Jessie Mae was bats. She looked at the woods and saw nothing but woods. She looked at Harriet, and when she saw Harriet only looking indignant as usual, she felt better.

"Come on and see," said Jessie Mae and rode her bike right into the woods.

Harriet followed, and looking down, Beth Ellen could see that there was the faintest suspicion of a path.

They rode on until they came to a small clearing. The sun hit the bald patch of dirt in an almost perfect circle. It looked as though designed for the light, as the light spots in some cathedrals look designed.

Oh, thought Beth Ellen, she only means it looks like a church.

Harriet leaned the bike against a tree. As Beth Ellen was clambering down, Harriet poked her and pointed to the clearing.

Jessie Mae was kneeling in the middle of the round patch. Her face was turned up to heaven and her hands were praying.

"Oh, dear," said Harriet, for once in awe. "What do we do now?"

Beth Ellen put her finger to her lips, signaling Harriet to be quiet. They waited for Jessie Mae to finish.

Jessie Mae was muttering to herself with her eyes closed. She finished finally, and getting up, looked around for them and smiled.

"Y'all come on in," she said sweetly. "This here's my church." They came into the light rather timidly.

"This the altar," she said proudly and showed them a wooden structure which was nailed to a tree on the edge of the clearing. It had a box on top and a box on the bottom. The box on top made a stand like an altar, and the box on the bottom held a Bible and two candles. Jessie Mae took out the Bible and put it on the altar. Then she took out the candles and stuck them in little knot holes on each side of the

Bible. Then she took out some matches and lit the candles.

"Did you build it yourself?" asked Harriet.

She can't think of anything else to say, thought Beth Ellen.

"Why, no," said Jessie Mae. "Norman helped me. We haven't got the robes worked out yet, but soon we gonna have those too."

"Robes?" Harriet's eyes were bugging.

"You know, vestments and things. We gonna have it all real fancy."

Beth Ellen found herself feeling a certain envy. I must have a profession, she thought hurriedly. I must decide. Everyone I know has something like this. Something to love. I need something to love.

"Let's go now," said Jessie Mae, putting away the candles and the Bible, "unless y'all want to pray a little."

Harriet ran for her bike.

"No, thank you," said Beth Ellen, suddenly wanting to say: I just ate. She turned and walked to the bike. She got into the basket and Harriet pushed her to the road, then got on and began following Jessie Mae again.

They rode up the little dirt road to The Preacher's house. It sat on a hill surrounded by dogwoods and snowball bushes.

"What a funny little house," said Harriet.

"It's a *real* nice house," said Jessie Mae with enthusiasm.

Beth Ellen looked the house over. It didn't look like any of the summer houses nor did it look like the farmers' houses around there. It looked like the kind of house she had seen in books about the South. There was a breezeway separating the two parts and through this you could see the trees and hills beyond. The two halves sat looking at each other as though in conversation. It looks like a friendly house, thought Beth Ellen.

"Get down," said Harriet, who was huffing up the hill. Beth Ellen got down and Harriet pushed the bike. Jessie Mae was going ahead fast, eagerly. When they got to the top, she was already starting up the steps.

"Well, well. Hi there, Jessie." The Preacher had come out onto the porch "My, my. You brought along the little rich critters, I see. Hi, y'all!" He waved his cane at Harriet and Beth Ellen.

"Hi, y'all," said Harriet. Beth Ellen poked her in the ribs.

"I can't help it," Harriet whispered irritably. "When someone talks like that, I can't help doing it."

"Hello," said Beth Ellen shyly.

"They wanted to meet you," said Jessie Mae.

"Me?" He raised his eyebrows. "Now who in the

world would want to meet *me?*"

Not knowing what to say, everyone stared at him.

"I tell y'all what," he said, hitting the porch with his cane to emphasize his idea, "I'm gonna make a pitcher of lemonade."

"Oh, goody," said Jessie Mae. "Can I help you?"

The Preacher turned and started for the door. "Naw, it's nothing. You sit down in the yard there with your friends. I won't be a minute." He disappeared inside.

Jessie Mae led the way across the bumpy yard to some chairs placed around a big round wicker table. "Here's where we sit all the time," she said happily and sat down.

"Can't we see inside?" asked Harriet.

Harriet's like a puppy, thought Beth Ellen. If she can't smell a new place all over, she isn't happy.

"No," said Jessie Mae. "He didn't ask us in, so we can't go in. He *asked* us *here.*"

"Have you ever been in?" asked Harriet.

"Yes, one time, to get a drink of water 'cause it was so hot riding over."

"What's it look like?" Harriet sat down unwillingly.

"Just a house," said Jessie Mae and shrugged.

"I sure would like a look around," said Harriet, craning toward the windows, "just to see if he's got some notes in there he hasn't used yet."

"What?" Jessie Mae looked astonished.

"The *notes*," Harriet squeaked, "like the ones you got in the garage! I don't know why I have to be the only one who can even *remember* the notes! Nobody seems to have a curious bone in their—"

"Oh, Harriet," Beth Ellen interrupted, "who *cares?*"

"*I* care," said Harriet and stood up resolutely, "and I'm going in there and look around."

"Listen, girl, you really think The Preacher would bother himself leaving notes around?"

"I'm *going*," said Harriet stubbornly and started toward the porch.

"Here we go." The Preacher came out of the door carrying a tray. "This oughta cool everything off. I got some those cookies you like too, Jessie." He came past Harriet and set the tray down on the table. Harriet turned around and sat down again docilely.

The pitcher of lemonade was frosted on the outside. Harriet started eating cookies as though she'd been starved all her life. Beth Ellen ate three, then stopped politely and watched them disappear down Harriet's throat like peanuts.

"Well, you like those, don't you, critter?" said The Preacher, laughing at Harriet. His teeth were long and yellow and his smile was warm. "Don't they feed you in that big rich house?"

229

Harriet almost choked. Jessie Mae began to laugh and Beth Ellen giggled.

"What are you laughing about, Mouse?" said Harriet when she could talk. "Your house is bigger than mine."

The Preacher and Jessie Mae turned to look at Beth Ellen. Beth Ellen looked at her feet.

"You a mouse, child?" asked The Preacher, chuckling. "Well, I wouldn't worry. The mice shall inherit the earth, it's said."

Jessie Mae fell to the ground laughing.

"AHA!" said Harriet, standing up and holding one finger in the air. "You SEE, he quotes things and also he quotes 'em funny, just like the note leaver!"

Beth Ellen looked at The Preacher. Jessie Mae stopped laughing and looked up from the ground. Harriet leaned across the table.

"I've got you now," she said ominously.

The Preacher looked startled, then laughed. "You mean that fella leaving things all over Water Mill? Well, I got to admit, that's where I got that little joke from. I saw that written on a little piece of paper. . . . I was there in Water Mill. I thought it's so funny I brought it home and I got it here inside . . . you want to see it?" He stood up.

"Sure, sure," said Harriet rudely, "a likely story. That's the easiest thing in the world to say, and then you just show us something you wrote. *I* know better.

If you've got a note like that *in your possession,* you're the *one.*"

"That's dumb, Harriet," said Beth Ellen in a tone very brisk for her. "Anyone who's been sent one has it in their possession."

The Preacher laughed at Harriet's reddening face. "Ain't such a mouse after all, are you?" he said to Beth Ellen. He sat down again. "I'm mighty interested myself in who'd do a thing like this. It must be a strange mind to think of taking the words of the Holy Bible and twisting them or just saying them with a mind to make people unhappy. As I understand, they are not pleasant notes." He looked at Harriet. "Of course I'm not running up and down the countryside playing detective, but I sure would like to know. People are getting pretty agitated about the situation. I hear they're of a mind, too, to catch the guilty party."

"Well," said Harriet, "finally! I'm glad somebody's interested. Why don't we catch him?"

"Well, like I said, I don't fancy myself a detective, but I'll give you what help I can."

"I'd like to see that note you have," said Harriet importantly.

"All righty!" He got up and went toward the porch, then turned back. "I *was* gonna give it to the police if they asked, but I reckon you'll do just as well." And with a crooked smile he went indoors.

"What did he mean by that?" asked Harriet.

"He means you're pompous. How can *you* ever catch anybody?" said Beth Ellen. Jessie Mae laughed.

"I don't care what you say . . . hey! He didn't say who *got* the note." Harriet was so engrossed that she stared at the house, waiting for The Preacher to emerge.

She doesn't even care when she's insulted, thought Beth Ellen.

"I reckon he'll tell you," said Jessie Mae.

"I like him," said Harriet. "At least he *cares* there's some maniac loose leaving notes. He seems like a nice old man."

"He is," said Jessie Mae stoutly.

"What makes you say the note leaver is a maniac?" asked Beth Ellen. "Janie said—"

"Never MIND what Janie said," Harriet shouted. "I think it's a maniac!"

"Here it is," said The Preacher, coming across the lawn and handing the small paper to Harriet. She looked at it as though she had X-ray eyes.

Jessie Mae looked over her shoulder. "Looks like all the others," she said and sat down again.

"It's a mystery," said The Preacher, "but there are a great many mysteries in this life."

"Where do you come from?" asked Harriet suddenly. Beth Ellen was astounded. Harriet has some nerve, she thought to herself; I'd never ask anyone anything.

"I come from the backwoods a long way away," said The Preacher slowly.

"He had his *own* church," said Jessie Mae with awe.

"What happened to it?" asked Harriet.

Jessie Mae looked shocked. "Well! I reckon that's The Preacher's business!"

"It don't matter, Jessie. The child's got a burden of curiosity. I don't mind trying to relieve anybody's burden." He settled himself in his chair and took a long sip of lemonade.

"Did you get fired?" Harriet asked eagerly.

"Of course he didn't get fired," said Jessie Mae furiously. "Listen here, you, you just like all Yankees. Not a *bit* of manners!"

Harriet looked amazed. Beth Ellen felt somehow joyous. There was a large silence. Jessie Mae continued to stand ready to run Harriet over Cemetery Ridge.

The Preacher laughed. "Well, now, Jessie, this little critter's got hold of the truth. I did get fired, in a sense."

"You DIDN'T," said Jessie Mae frantically. "*You* told the truth and the Elders came and told you you were replaced. *They* were wrong!"

"Nobody was wrong." The Preacher spoke so sternly that they all snapped their heads around to look at him. He held their attention one strange moment by his fierce expression, then he laughed. "God fired me, maybe, but for good reason."

"He did *not*. He wouldn't have! You weren't BAD!" Jessie Mae screamed.

The Preacher laughed. "I was a bad preacher, Jessie." He put his lemonade glass down carefully on the table. "A good preacher should be able to help. I wanted to help them . . ."

Beth Ellen looked at his long teeth and suddenly liked him immensely. He's not afraid, she thought; he's not afraid of anyone.

"But it's gonna be all right," interrupted Jessie Mae nervously. "You're thinking it all out and when you're ready you'll go back. That's what you said." She looked strangely appealing as she stood there leaning toward him hopefully.

"You know, Jessie," began The Preacher, leaning back in his chair, "you from my part of the country. You know what a sharecropper's life is like. You know how the migrant workers live—"

"How? How?" interrupted Harriet wildly.

She can't bear not to know everything, thought Beth Ellen.

The Preacher laughed. "I'll put it to you this way, little curious Yankee. Just about the only way they can get through this world is to think there's another one coming up."

Jessie Mae sat down with a bump. "You mean you don't think there's another one?" she gasped out.

"Even if there is, Jessie, why does this one have to be so bad?" The Preacher asked calmly.

There was a long silence. Beth Ellen felt the heavy air, the air before a rain, touch her face like a gloved hand. They all looked at The Preacher's solemn face, his warm eyes. The wind rustled the old trees.

"But . . ." Beth Ellen found herself talking without ever planning to. "The meek shall inherit . . . like you said." She suddenly heard her own voice and fell into anguished silence.

Harriet looked at Beth Ellen long and hard. Beth Ellen felt it and looked up. She jumped when she saw Harriet's eyes.

"You can tell them that for only so long," said The Preacher quietly. "There comes a time when they're tired of waiting."

I am tired, thought Beth Ellen.

"And you can tell the rich about the eye of the needle, and they only get richer." The Preacher looked up at the trees in disgust.

"But the Good Book . . ." said Jessie Mae. Beth Ellen looked at the consternation on that freckled face and felt sad.

The Preacher leaned forward and looked right into

Jessie Mae's eyes. "Religion is a tool, Jessie, just like a tractor or a shovel or a pitchfork. It is a tool to get through life with. And if it works, it is a good tool. And if it don't work, it is a bad tool. Now, for my people there it don't work."

"But . . ." began Jessie Mae.

"There's got to be a new tool," said The Preacher. He settled back in his chair.

"But it's a good tool," said Jessie Mae. She seemed about to cry.

"For you . . . for me." The Preacher looked gentle. "But not for everyone."

"But they—" began Jessie Mae determinedly.

"They are tired of waiting," said The Preacher flatly.

I am tired of waiting, thought Beth Ellen.

"But . . . what you gonna do?" asked Jessie Mae.

"It's not what *I'm* gonna do," said The Preacher smiling. "It's what *you* all are gonna do. It's *you* all inheriting this old world in the mess it's in. What *you* gonna do?"

Jessie Mae's mouth dropped open. Beth Ellen looked at The Preacher, then back at Jessie Mae.

"Well . . . we'll FIX it," said Harriet.

The Preacher laughed a long time. "That's the ticket," he said finally. "I'd like to see the world you three make." He laughed again, as though he were happy.

Harriet was looking at Beth Ellen again. "HEY!" she said suddenly, and turned to The Preacher. "Who got that note about the mice?"

"I did," said The Preacher smiling. "And whoever sent it . . ."—he looked around and his eye fell on Beth Ellen—"whoever sent it was right. There's a lot of mouse in me."

Beth Ellen dropped her glass. It fell on her sneaker and sloshed lemonade up her leg. She turned red and leaned over to pick it up.

"That's all right. It didn't break," said Jessie Mae.

Beth Ellen put the empty glass back on the table. When she looked up, she met Harriet's eyes. Harriet was leaning forward staring at her with intense concentration.

"Well, chickens, I've enjoyed this," said The Preacher, and without another word, he got up and loped toward his house.

I like that, thought Beth Ellen. He doesn't waste a lot of time on foolishness. When he wants to go, he just leaves.

"*Very interesting,*" said Harriet looking at Beth Ellen.

"What's the matter with you?" asked Beth Ellen, feeling irritated.

"Nice to meet y'all," yelled The Preacher from his porch.

"Nice to meet you," called Harriet and Beth Ellen

in unison. They looked at Jessie Mae, who was quiet.

"Let's go," said Harriet.

Jessie Mae stood up, ran down the hill, jumped on her bike, and was away before anyone could say a word. They watched her, then got up and walked slowly down the hill.

Beth Ellen climbed into the basket. She could feel Harriet's eyes boring into the back of her neck all the way home.

CHAPTER 22

Early the next morning Beth Ellen sat in bed reading her favorite book. She had awakened with a feeling of excitement the cause of which she was at first unable to determine. Then she remembered that today was the day Zeeney and Wallace were supposed to find out about their tickets. Today they would set their day of departure. She had determined to give them another chance before they left.

She hopped out of bed, hid her book away, and pulled on a pair of shorts and an old blue sweater. She could always wear what she wanted until noon these days, but after that she was told. The obscure places that Zeeney and Wallace insisted upon taking her always demanded some bizarre costume. Why anyone would want to go to those places was a mystery to her, like the fashion show poolside at the Bath and Tennis. Beth Ellen always sat stiffly in mummified boredom, afraid to move, to speak, to spill.

She ran down the hall to the back steps. She would never take the front steps on a dark morning. The frights along that route were too many to be endured, from the great brown varnished painting of the nymphs and satyr to the white sculpture whose arms extended unexpectedly from the niche like the grasping arms of a ghost. She ran past the wide steps and reached the narrow back stairs quite out of breath.

She bolted into the warmth of the kitchen, almost sighing with relief at the ordinary postures of the maid, the cook at the stove, the slouching chauffeur reading his paper. She said nothing but went up and stood next to the cook, Sarah.

"There you are," said Sarah cheerfully. "Ready for your breakfast?"

Beth Ellen nodded. She walked through the kitchen into the breakfast room. She sat down and unfolded her napkin. I am all alone, she thought.

She looked out the window toward the summerhouse. Zeeney and Wallace were having breakfast there. Zeeney wore a long yellow peignoir and Wallace had on white flannels and an orange jacket. They were posed like a Victorian greeting card.

Zeeney's lips were moving constantly as she slit open the mail savagely with a long silver letter-opener. Beth Ellen watched her lips move and was grateful she couldn't hear.

Her breakfast was brought in. She ate it slowly, never taking her eyes away from the window. I may run away, she thought in a lazy way, and remembered the time she *had* run away. She had been four years old and it had been out here because it was summer. They had found her a mile down the road carrying a suitcase full of washrags. Everyone had laughed and asked, Why washrags? She hadn't had the faintest idea. She had simply gone to the linen closet and packed what fit best. It had been a very small suitcase.

I won't run away, she thought, chewing bacon. I had better find a profession, then I can be independent and not like Zeeney. She finished her breakfast and slid off the chair. With a certain mad look in her eye she ran through the sunroom, through the small garden, out onto the lawn, and to the summerhouse.

"Good MORN-ING, dar-ling!" Zeeney's voice swept over her like a broom. Wallace looked up, gave her a bored look, and went back to his paper. Beth Ellen sat down.

"Mother," she said loudly.

Zeeney looked behind her, then realized Beth Ellen must mean her. "Oh!" she said brightly, "YES, dear." She hates the very word, thought Beth Ellen.

"Mother, what profession should I be?" Beth Ellen's voice, for some reason, was getting louder and louder.

"PRO-FES-SION?" Zeeney screamed as though she'd been pinched.

"Yes." For the first time in her life Beth Ellen felt absolutely triumphant.

Zeeney looked at her aghast. Even Wallace twisted around in his chair and gave her a red-eyed stare. They looked, then, at each other.

They started to laugh. They burst into gales of rocking guffaws. They shook and quivered and screeched and howled and grabbed each other across the table.

That does it, thought Beth Ellen; that is the answer. When they had subsided somewhat, Zeeney squeaked out, laughing into each word, "Well, dear, what about weight lifting?"

Very funny, thought Beth Ellen.

"Or"—and Wallace broke himself right up—"you could apply to the Sleeping Car Porters' Union. There must be openings." They grabbed each other and rocked back and forth. "If you don't mind the travel," he finished, flinging Zeeney into a gasping hysteria.

You are two very funny people, thought Beth Ellen. You are so funny that I am going out and get a job as a plumber.

She sat stoically through their outburst. She sat on, unmoved, through suggestions that she get a seat on the stock exchange; be the first woman to climb Mount Everest; take up log rolling, sewer cleaning; be a sailor; get to be mayor of New York, and of course the first woman President. The last threatened to give them both apoplexy.

She sat quite still. Her stillness finally reached them. They dried their eyes and looked at her. Wallace went "Heh, heh, heh" and returned to his paper. I could choke him to death, thought Beth Ellen. Zeeney looked at her a long time, then sat up briskly as though she had made a decision.

"You will, of course, finish your schooling, take a year in Europe, return to New York, make your debut, and marry." She looked at Beth Ellen with absolute certainty. There was more, in fact, than certainty in those eyes. There was an unspoken command which, if flaunted, would cause whole generations to come down out of the paintings on the walls and lead her by the hand to some secret dungeon.

"I thought I might be an artist," said Beth Ellen staunchly.

"Preposterous," said Zeeney.

"I can draw," said Beth Ellen.

"So what?" said Zeeney.

"I draw the best in my class."

"You have no talent. Believe me, we would have heard by now if you had. At your age Michelangelo had painted the Sistine Chapel."

"That's not true!" said Beth Ellen, incensed.

"Well, it will serve to prove my point."

"But I want to."

"Ridiculous. Forget it."

"I might be good."

"FORGET it. Pretend you never thought of it."

"Harriet is going to be a writer."

"Who is Harriet? Don't bother me with your petty little friends and their aspirations. I *know* what *you* will be."

"How?"

"Because *I* will decide, how else?"

Oh, no, you won't, thought Beth Ellen. One more try.

"Harriet M. Welsch. You met her the other night."

"You don't mean Rodger Welsch's child? Be a writer? What an extremely tacky thing to say. It must be the child's mother, because Rodger was never that way. You *must* learn, dear girl, that it's tacky to say you're going to be *anything*, except, of course, *rich*, which you *will* be. Now let's hear no more about it."

"I'm going to college and get a Ph.D." Beth Ellen felt a desperation come into her voice.

"You'll do nothing of the sort. You will attend a suitable school, for two years at the *most*. A school that *I* shall pick."

"Then I'll leave and be an artist." Beth Ellen stood up.

"My dear child, you haven't the faintest idea how revolting you're being. Now if you'll leave us in peace, I'll be charitable and forget you ever ran off at the mouth like this." She waved Beth Ellen away.

Beth Ellen walked across the lawn. That settles it, she thought. Anything that Zeeney dislikes that much has got to be good.

She sat down on the little bench in the garden and leaned her head back. Zeeney was looking curiously at her across the long lawn. Beth Ellen didn't care now that she was being looked at. Besides, she knew that Zeeney was blind as a bat and refused to wear glasses because she was vain. That's it, thought Beth Ellen: Never be afraid to wear glasses.

She luxuriated in the sun. I am going someplace, she thought. One day I will be somebody and nobody will laugh at me. Nobody will ever laugh at me again.

CHAPTER 23

The next morning Beth Ellen presented herself at the summerhouse for breakfast.

"What's this?" asked Zeeney, looking her over.

"I'm going to eat breakfast with you," said Beth Ellen.

"Oh," said Zeeney in a false voice, "how *very* nice." She turned back to her mail which sat on a small silver plate. "I hope you don't spill or chew loudly, because it would upset Wallace."

Beth Ellen tried to look like someone who chewed softly. When she had gotten up that morning, she had wanted to come to breakfast because for some reason she had felt free, as though they couldn't touch her, as though nothing they said could unnerve her in any way. Her thought had been that it would be fun just to watch them and know they couldn't do anything to her.

Wallace came across the lawn and up the steps to sit down. He noticed Beth Ellen. "Good morning," he said politely. The maid came and set another place at the table.

"What's in the mail, dear? Hup?" asked Wallace as he unfolded his paper.

"Cartier's."

"Oh?"

"A bill."

"Oh," said Wallace softly.

"What's this?" Zeeney asked herself, and Beth Ellen craned her neck to see what Zeeney had found.

Breakfast arrived as Zeeney slit the long envelope. She looked at what was inside.

"Well!" she screamed, "Agatha has gone too far!"

Wallace jumped, then said, "What? What? What is it?"

Beth Ellen tried to see but couldn't.

"What? Hup? What?" Wallace was choking a little.

"Here! See for yourself," said Zeeney furiously and passed the paper to Wallace. It went by Beth Ellen an inch from her nose, so she couldn't see anything.

"HUP!" said Wallace angrily.

"Indecent!" said Zeeney. "How can *she* talk with both her children in the nut house? Typical!"

"Hup."

"I'd like to go over there and smash her wax face in. She's had so many face lifts that if you set a match to her she'd melt. Paraffin witch."

"Wouldn't go smash her, dear," said Wallace and laughed as though he'd made a witticism.

"May I see it?" asked Beth Ellen politely.

"Absolutely not. *Not* for children," said Zeeney crossly.

"I don't see why not," said Wallace. "It's just silliness." He handed it to Beth Ellen.

She looked at the red printing:

HOW SHARPER THAN A SERPENT'S TOOTH
IS A ROTTEN PARENT

She laughed.

"WALLACE!" screamed Zeeney, "a *child* should not be exposed to such things."

"Hup! *King Lear*."

"I couldn't care less. Sometimes you have absolutely no sense." Zeeney snatched the paper from Beth Ellen, balled it up, and threw it out onto the middle of the lawn where it lay, a wounded paper bird.

Zeeney went back to her mail. She crossed and un-

crossed her legs a number of times and lit a ciga-
rette. Wallace went back to his paper.

Beth Ellen ate her breakfast. I must call Harriet,
she thought, and tell her about this.

"AHA!" said Zeeney. Beth Ellen looked up.
Zeeney looked like a witch who had finished her
cauldron soup.

"Here, DAR-LING," she said pointedly and passed
him an envelope. It was long with red printing on the
front.

"What?" said Wallace and absently took the note.
He opened it while still reading the newspaper. He
pulled out a small piece of paper.

"Well!" he said when he had read it. "I can't see
why she should send that to *me!*"

He handed it to Zeeney. Zeeney read it and
laughed like a maniac. Wallace looked furious and
red. Zeeney laughed harder.

Always laughing, thought Beth Ellen; always
laughing *at* someone. "May I see it?" she asked.

"Absolutely not," said Wallace.

"Of course," said Zeeney excitedly and handed it
to Beth Ellen. Wallace dove for the note but couldn't
get it. He scurried behind the newspaper.

Beth Ellen read:

HE THAT MAKETH HASTE TO BE RICH
SHALL NOT BE INNOCENT

251

Beth Ellen giggled. She couldn't help it.

Zeeney laughed pleasantly, pleased with herself. "Agatha," she said pointedly, "is no fool."

Beth Ellen excused herself and ran into the house. She got to the phone as fast as she could and called Harriet.

"Oh, *tell*, quick!" said Harriet.

Beth Ellen told her.

"And were they written in exactly the same way?" asked Harriet in a *very* detective voice.

"Yes."

"I wish we could get that paper analyzed."

"What does that mean?"

"Then we could tell where the person bought it. If only I were on the police force."

Beth Ellen had a vision of Harriet in uniform.

"What did Zeeney say when she read it?"

"She thinks Agatha Plumber sent them."

"She's wrong," said Harriet in a curious voice.

"What do you mean?"

"Because I *know* who's been sending 'em," said Harriet in a voice like a snake.

"WHAT?" Beth Ellen heard herself scream. "WHO?"

"I'm not talking."

"Aw, come on, Harriet, who is it?"

"I can't say until I have all my information in. I think I'll run along now."

"HARRIET! *Tell* me!"

"The work must go on. Have to go now."

"Harriet, you're impossible. *Tell me.*"

"Signing off," said Harriet in her most infuriating way and hung up abruptly.

Beth Ellen slammed the phone down and looked up to see the maid looking at her strangely.

"Your grandmother wants to see you," she said.

"Okay," said Beth Ellen. "Thanks," she added absently.

She walked down the hall to her grandmother's room. Mrs. Hansen looked up at her with a curious hawklike eye and a faint smile.

Beth Ellen sat down on the chaise across from the bed.

"How is it going?" Mrs. Hansen seemed to be repressing a laugh.

"What?" Beth Ellen still felt such irritation at Harriet that she could feel little else.

"The visit."

"Visit?" Beth Ellen felt like a fog on the road.

"Your mother . . . and Wallace . . . how are you getting on?"

"Oh, that."

"Yes, *that.* How is it going?"

"Well . . ." said Beth Ellen thinking: What can I say? . . . I want to flush them both down a toilet?

"I see . . ." said her grandmother, as though she

could read minds. She turned her face toward the window. The light made a soft line along her nose. "I know my daughter, after all. I thought perhaps her travels . . . I thought she might have grown, have learned a bit." She turned briskly toward Beth Ellen. "But she hasn't changed a whit. She is just as silly as ever; a silly woman who contributes nothing whatever to life. She might as well not be alive except that she consumes. That's all she does. She consumes . . . food, clothing, shelter, seats on airplanes, and people." She looked steadily at Beth Ellen.

Beth Ellen looked steadily back.

"I will not let her consume you."

Beth Ellen's eyes widened.

"You don't seem to understand, child. Zeeney feels you're under some bad influence here. She says you've talked to her about a profession. . . ." She hesitated and smiled at Beth Ellen. "I think it's an admirable thing to be thinking of, but you must remember something"—she smiled again—"and that is that there is nothing the chic hate quite so much as the thought of work." She looked out the window again. "I think it probably turns their stomachs." She looked back at Beth Ellen. "So, because your brain and heart have been poisoned . . ." She looked at Beth Ellen expectantly.

Beth Ellen looked back at her.

254

"I don't think you understand, child; she wants to take you with her."

Beth Ellen felt rather than heard the scream tear from her throat. She banged the door after her and felt the slap-slap of her shoes on the hall floor and she ran, ran wildly, ran zigzag, ran as though chased by her grandmother's cries of "Child, child" floating after her.

She ran into her room and slammed the door as hard as she could. She ran into her bathroom and slammed the door as hard as she could. As she slammed the bathroom door she thought, That is the third door I have ever slammed in my life. I don't care. I don't care anymore. I will slam every door I run into for the rest of my life. She ran up and down the bathroom. She couldn't stop.

It isn't fair, it isn't fair, it isn't fair, ran through her head. I'm not a child, she thought with a wild scream in her head. I never was a child and now I'm really not. I'm going from a troll to an old woman. It isn't fair.

It isn't fair, it isn't fair. Before she knew it, before she even heard her own voice, she was screaming at the top of her lungs and throwing everything in sight. She started with the towels, which she tried to tear up and couldn't. She broke the glass sitting on the sink. She threw her toothbrush on the floor and

255

stepped on it, grinding her heel in. She tried to pick up the scale and throw it through the window, but it was too heavy, and she dropped it on the tiles where it made a satisfying, resounding, thundering crash.

Then she opened the door and slammed it. She opened it again and slammed it again. She didn't even know what she was doing. It's not fair. It's not fair. It's not fair. She heard only that. Over and over and over. The slamming door rang out like punctuation— a big, bang period at the end of each phrase.

She stopped that and ran over and turned on the shower. Then she turned the nozzle of the shower so the spray hit the floor.

Through the water she ran into her room. She threw everything on the dresser across the room. Then she opened the door to her room and slammed it. The water was now pouring out of the bathroom into her room. She slammed the door again. She slammed it three times and the fourth time she opened it there were Zeeney, Wallace, and the maid. She got only a glimpse of their three startled faces before she slammed it again, plunged through the cascading water into the bathroom, and locked the door.

They started banging on the bathroom door. Beth Ellen sat down on the tub and pretended she was sitting under Niagara Falls. She hugged her knees. I will flood the house, she thought. Then I will begin to grow and be huge. I will get so monstrously big that I will break the bathroom out and fill the house, the yard, all of Water Mill. I will tower over the Montauk Highway like a colossus. They will all run away like ants.

The cold water ran down on her, on her head, her clothes. It beat around her ears like the safe rain of a summer's day.

The chauffeur broke the door down. Zeeney congratulated him, as did Wallace, before they thought to run into the bathroom. The maid and chauffeur picked Beth Ellen up off the floor because neither Zeeney nor Wallace wanted to get wet. The maid put her on the bed and started to undress her. Wallace and Harry went out. The maid took off the wet clothes and put warm pajamas on Beth Ellen while Zeeney stood there saying things like "What's got into you?" "You're a spoiled brat. Imagine, a tantrum like that!" and "You'll learn a thing or two, just wait and see!" She finished with "Best thing for a tantrum is to just let someone scream their head off and not pay a jot of attention," and having offered this brilliant solution, she turned on her heel and swished from the room.

The maid dried Beth Ellen's hair. It stood up in great bouncing curls. It's me. It's my hair, thought Beth Ellen.

When she was all warm and dry and tucked into bed, the maid brought her a cup of hot chocolate and then opened the door very wide. "There's someone here to see you," she said, and through the door came her grandmother in her wheelchair.

"Hello, darling," she said, and Beth Ellen burst into tears. Her grandmother came close to the bed and Beth Ellen leaned way out and put her head down in her lap. She cried until she thought she could never stop. Her grandmother patted her hair and leaned down to kiss her many times.

CHAPTER 24

The next morning when Beth Ellen woke up she felt wonderful. When she remembered what had happened the day before, she felt a hundred years old. Her grandmother had said she wanted to talk to her in the morning, and remembering that, she felt afraid. I certainly was no lady, she thought to herself.

She got out of bed and was surprised to feel stiff. She pulled on her shorts. I want to get it over with, she thought, before breakfast. She opened her door and went down the hall.

"Come in," her grandmother sang out when she knocked on the door. She doesn't *sound* mad, Beth Ellen thought. She went in.

"Good morning, darling. Sit down." Her grandmother was reading the morning paper. She looked extraordinarily cheerful.

Beth Ellen sat down. Her grandmother looked at her. She looked back.

"How do you feel this morning?" asked Mrs. Hansen.

"Okay," said Beth Ellen.

Mrs. Hansen folded her paper and took off her reading glasses. "I've thought a great deal about yesterday, as I'm sure you have too." Mrs. Hansen seemed to get embarrassed suddenly, because she looked out the window. "But we'll talk about that in a minute." She turned and looked directly into Beth Ellen's eyes. Over the hawk nose the large eyes were violet in the morning light. "You're very timid, aren't you?"

"What?" Beth Ellen was caught completely unaware.

Her grandmother looked away. "I suppose you're timid because you've had to grow up here with an old lady. You haven't had any real life. But there's something I want to tell you about timidity, about shyness."

Beth Ellen searched her grandmother's face to see if she were angry, but the face looked impassive. I'm going to be told I'm bad, she thought.

"Shy people are angry people," said Mrs. Hansen

and snapped her head around to see Beth Ellen's reaction.

I am not a lady, thought Beth Ellen. It's coming now. She's going to say I am not a lady.

"You know," said her grandmother, smiling, "it's important to be a lady, but not if you lose everything else, not if you lose yourself in the process."

Beth Ellen felt her mouth drop open.

"There are times when we *must* express what we feel even if it is anger. If you can feel it and not express it . . . it might be better, but you *must* try to know what you feel. If we don't know what we feel, we get into trouble." She looked hard at Beth Ellen. "You're a very angry little girl. I have no idea what you've been doing about it because you've never shown any of it before yesterday, to my knowledge."

Beth Ellen turned pale.

Mrs. Hansen looked away, took a deep breath, then looked back.

"Now," she said slowly, "would you like to tell me whether you want to go to Europe with Zeeney or not?"

"I wouldn't go to the corner with Zeeney." This burst out so loudly that Beth Ellen sat in total astonishment, listening to it float across the room. I'll be killed, she thought.

It took a second for her grandmother to realize what had been said but when she did she laughed the

261

biggest, most enchanting laugh Beth Ellen had ever heard. She continued to laugh for a little while and then she said, "Well! I don't think I've ever heard a more honest statement." She wiped her eyes and smiled across the bed. "And I can't tell you how happy I am to hear it. It's settled then. You'll live with me and I'm very glad."

She smiled so sweetly that Beth Ellen got up and ran across the room. Her grandmother held out her arms and gave her a big hug. Her grandmother held her away from her and they laughed together as though they shared a secret.

"Can I ask Harriet to spend the night?" Beth Ellen asked rapidly.

"Of course, darling. I think they've disrupted our lives quite enough, don't you think? It's time we got back to normal. Ask her for tonight."

"And I don't have to go to the Bath and Tennis anymore?"

"As far as I'm concerned"—her grandmother laughed—"you don't ever have to go there again for the rest of your life."

"HOORAY!" Beth Ellen yelled, hugged her grandmother and ran out of the room. I sound just like Harriet, she thought as she ran along the hall; and then wildly in her head rang over and over again the phrase, I live somewhere, I live somewhere, I live somewhere.

She dialed Harriet's number.

"HI, HARRIET," she said loudly.

"Who is this?" said Harriet suspiciously.

"BETH ELLEN!" She shouted it. It was fun to talk loud, she discovered.

"Well, don't break my eardrum," said Harriet grumpily, then cleverly: "Are you *sure* you're Beth Ellen? You don't sound like her a bit. Say, what is this? Who is this?"

Beth Ellen laughed. "It's me. Listen, can you come spend the night?"

"Sure. Well, I mean, I don't know; I have to ask."

"Well, ASK, stupid." Beth Ellen felt her heart race with glee.

"All right, all right," grumbled Harriet and let the phone clatter out of her hands. Feet stomped away.

Beth Ellen stood humming. She saw her secret book peeking out from under the bed and she kicked it across the room. "Who needs you?" she yelled.

"What?" said Harriet. "Listen, Beth Ellen, are you drunk?"

"No." Beth Ellen giggled. "Can you come?"

"Yes. When?"

"For dinner. We can have it in front of the television."

"Have the creeps left?"

"They're *leaving*," yelled Beth Ellen, "and I'm staying *here*."

"Of course you are, silly; you live there."

"Come over at five," said Beth Ellen and hung up, blissful that she hadn't even said good-bye. Oh, Harriet, she thought as she walked away, for all your spying how *little* you know.

Zeeney was coming up the steps. She snapped her fingers at Beth Ellen. "Get into your yellow dress. We're going to brunch at the Bath and Tennis; although, after that performance yesterday, I don't know why I take you anywhere."

Beth Ellen's heart raced. "You're *not* taking me anywhere," she said simply.

"What?" said Zeeney as though a chair had spoken.

Beth Ellen snapped her fingers right in Zeeney's face. "I'm not going," she said loudly. "I'm not going *anywhere* with *you!*"

Zeeney's mouth dropped open and Beth Ellen laughed, turned on her heel, went to the front steps, and without looking back, slid down the banister, down past the grinning satyr, down past the ghost sculpture, past the family portraits—sour face by sour face, one by one—down and down until she landed with a bump at the end. She looked up at Zeeney's astonished face looking over the banister, gave a great whoop of laughter, jumped off, and ran with all her might.

CHAPTER 25

After dinner that night Beth Ellen and Harriet were
watching television. Beth Ellen was switching from
channel to channel, which meant back and forth between two, looking for something good when Harriet
said, "I hate television."

"I like it," said Beth Ellen smartly.

"It's dumb," said Harriet, her mouth full of popcorn. She grabbed the television program and looked
it over in disgust. "Look at these things. Look at all
these dumb people. Look at these rotten things. I
never saw such dumb things. There isn't *anything* I'd
like to see. There's *never* anything I'd like to see.
What a bunch of ridiculous . . . HEY!" she suddenly

yelled. "There's a GREAT Nazi movie on!"

She turned to Beth Ellen, who was flipping channels like a zombie.

"Quick," she screamed, "turn it to that!" She leapt across the room.

Beth Ellen looked over her shoulder at the program, then turned to the right channel. Some Nazis were beating up an old woman on the street.

"Look at those rotten things! Oh, boy!" said Harriet and sat down, stuffing a great gob of popcorn in her mouth.

Beth Ellen glanced at Harriet. Harriet had been strange ever since she walked in the door. First of all she had looked at Beth Ellen with narrowed eyes and said, "Think I'm stupid, don't you?" Beth Ellen had said No, but it hadn't stopped Harriet from nodding her head and looking very mysterious. Beth Ellen had decided to ignore her. When they had gone into Beth Ellen's room, Harriet had begun opening closets, dresser drawers, and everything in sight as though she were looking for something. "What are you doing?" Beth Ellen had asked, and Harriet had replied, "You'll see! Think I don't know anything, don't you?"

After a great deal of looking around, the fit seemed to pass and Harriet had settled down to dinner and television.

"Rotten things, rotten Nazis . . . Hey! Something

266

about this reminds me of Norman and Jessie Mae," said Harriet through the popcorn.

"What do you mean?" asked Beth Ellen politely even though, truth be told, she couldn't have cared less.

"WELL," said Harriet as though she were just waiting for someone to ask her that, "*I* stopped by the Shark's Tooth Inn today!"

Beth Ellen cringed at the name as at an embarrassing memory.

"So?" she said, a bit truculantly. She looked at Harriet. Harriet looked as though she were waiting to have the information pulled out of her.

"AND . . . everything is *completely* different!" Harriet's eyes were glistening with the suspense she thought she was creating.

"*Hmmm,*" said Beth Ellen and looked at the television. Two can play at this, she thought.

"Well! Don't you even want to know?"

"Not particularly."

"You're impossible, Beth Ellen; not one shred of curiosity in your whole body."

"Did it ever occur to you that I don't CARE about anybody there?"

"Bunny?"

"Not anymore."

"*Hmmm.* Well, anyway, he quit and there isn't even any piano player. And Jessie Mae has changed all her plans. I saw her there because Norman had a wreck."

Beth Ellen continued to look at the television.

"You're infuriating. I don't care. I'm going to tell you anyway. Some man made Norman go get his car, and guess what?"

"What?" said Beth Ellen in as bored a voice as she could manage.

"Norman can't drive!"

"So?"

"So he got in the car and started it and drove round and round a tree and round and round the yard, and everybody was screaming and jumping out of the way, and he went round the hotel three times before he ran into that big hedge!"

Beth Ellen was looking at Harriet now.

"And Jessie Mae was there and she started yelling at Norman soon as the car stopped, and that old smelly Norman got out and, boy, did he look red. And the guy who owned the car was mad as a snake and said he was gonna sue Norman and Norman ran. Then Moo-Moo bit him."

"Bit him?" Beth Ellen laughed.

"Yeah, and made Norman stop running. And Jessie Mae was yelling her head off and she told Norman he was dumb and nasty because he didn't care about anything but money and she wasn't gonna have anything to do with him anymore and that he could forget all about the church because she was throwing over the whole idea and going to go to school and learn something else because she wasn't gonna make toe medicine either because it was dumb." Harriet stopped for breath. "Then Agatha Plumber comes waltzing in and said, 'DAR-LING, don't worry about a thing!' to the man whose car was smashed and took him off to her house for lunch. Then Norman ran like blazes and Jessie Mae ran after him still yelling at him." Harriet finished with a flourish and sat like a puppy waiting for a reward.

"*Hmmmm,*" said Beth Ellen.

"Oh, boy!" said Harriet. She flopped back in her chair, stuffed her mouth with popcorn, and watched the movie. "I'm never gonna tell you anything anymore," she said, popcorn flying out of her mouth as she spoke.

"I wonder if we'll ever see them again?" said Beth Ellen.

"Who?"

"Jessie Mae and Norman."

"Well, we could find out where they're gonna live in New York. What do you care, anyway? You don't care. I'm never gonna tell you another thing."

Beth Ellen smiled to herself. Imagine Harriet with her mouth shut permanently, she thought.

"You never tell *me* anything," said Harriet.

"What do you mean?" asked Beth Ellen, thinking: True, I don't.

"I know, I know," Harriet grumbled. "You think I don't know something, but I do."

"What?"

"Never mind. I'm not saying until . . ."

"Until what?"

"Until . . ." said Harriet, getting up, her eyes still glued on the television, "until I can PROVE it." She suddenly shouted the last and ran out of the room. Beth Ellen stood up, dumbfounded, and when she heard great crashing noises coming from her bedroom, she ran after.

Harriet was going through everything again and looking under the bed, in the bathroom, everywhere.

"What are you doing?" asked Beth Ellen in horror.

"Never mind, never mind," said Harriet and ran out of the room. She ran down the hall. She ran into the small sitting room and started looking there.

Beth Ellen ran after her. "What are you doing?" she yelled, but nothing had any effect upon Harriet, who searched everywhere like a mad thing. She ran out into the hall and toward Mrs. Hansen's room.

"Oh, no, you don't," said Beth Ellen and caught her just as her hand was about to touch the doorknob. "My grandmother's in there," she whispered.

"*Oh,*" said Harriet loudly and careened down the hall to Zeeney's room.

"Hey," said Beth Ellen and ran after.

Harriet did the same thing all over again—every drawer, every closet. "What are you looking for?" yelled Beth Ellen, but Harriet was off again and running. She ran into the room that had belonged to Beth Ellen's grandfather. Beth Ellen ran after her down the hall and heard Harriet shout "AHA!"

She ran into the room. Harriet was standing in front of the open Bible, one arm raised in triumph. "AHA!" she screamed again. "I've got you! I *knew* it was you! I just *knew it!*"

"What?" said Beth Ellen, her face paling.

"The Bible. You've got this Bible. You're the one. *You're* the note leaver!"

"Oh, rats, Harriet, that's silly. Everybody has a Bible. And anyway, wouldn't it be marked, where all those notes came from? Wouldn't it be marked?"

Harriet looked taken aback. "Maybe," she said slowly and looked at Beth Ellen. She hated for Beth Ellen to think of something she hadn't thought of. She looked at Beth Ellen with narrowed eyes.

Beth Ellen turned red. Harriet's eyes got even smaller and never left Beth Ellen's face.

Beth Ellen's eyes betrayed her. They roamed the room for one quick look. It only took a split second, but it was enough for Harriet, who followed the look and saw what Beth Ellen had seen. She ran across the room and dove under the bed.

She came up with Beth Ellen's secret book in her hand. "AHA!" she said and shook away a dust mouse hanging from her ear.

Beth Ellen began to shake.

"AHA, HA, HA!" said Harriet fiendishly. She turned the book over and looked at the title: *"Bartlett's Familiar Quotations?"* She looked at Beth Ellen in dismay. "What is that? I thought this was a Bible."

Beth Ellen took a deep breath. "It belonged to my grandfather," she gasped.

"What'd he do, keep his books under the bed?" Harriet snapped. She opened the book. A red crayon which had been holding the place fell out.

"AHA!" she screamed again. Beth Ellen jumped for the book. Harriet snatched it away and began to look with wild delight at the quotations encircled with red. "Oh, I SEE!" she yelled. "HERE's where you got them! Yep, uh-huh . . . uh-huh." She lowered the book and looked at Beth Ellen.

Beth Ellen felt the color drain from her face.

"You sure kept THAT secret a long time," said Harriet. "Why didn't you TELL me? I mean, you could have told me. Here I go around all summer

273

looking like a fool when you knew all along. WELL!"

Somehow Harriet's grumbling, so much a part of her, so much a part of everyday life, restored Beth Ellen. She began to breathe again. So what? she thought. I'm never gonna do it again anyway. So what if she knows? . . . She shrugged.

"Well, REALLY, Beth Ellen," said Harriet.

"You sound like Agatha Plumber," said Beth Ellen and laughed.

"I do NOT," said Harriet, furious. She started out of the room, still holding the book. "I'm seizing this as evidence," she said over her shoulder as she stomped into Beth Ellen's room. Beth Ellen followed. "And anyway, I think you should be prevented from doing this anymore!" Harriet looked at her.

I don't have to anymore, thought Beth Ellen.

"What ever gave you the idea to do it anyway?" asked Harriet with not a little admiration in her voice.

Beth Ellen smiled and said nothing.

"Well, you could have told me," said Harriet. "I knew it at The Preacher's. I watched your face and I knew. But you *could* have told me." And flinging the book on the bed, she stomped into the bathroom.

Beth Ellen sat on the bed and looked fondly at the book. I'm a child, she thought happily, and I live somewhere. Nobody can ever take me away.

Beth Ellen laughed, a loud, happy laugh.

"WHAT ARE YOU LAUGHING ABOUT?" yelled Harriet from behind the closed door. "Wait'll you read the story I'm gonna write about *you* and *those notes!*"

Beth Ellen laughed again. It didn't matter.

Secrets. Secrets.
It's no lie.
She writes them in her
notebook, 'ole

HARRIET
THE SPY

And they're a howl—the notebooks, the secrets, and, of course, Harriet. Read all about this zany, outspoken imp who just can't keep her pencil still. She's always writing *something*, which will make you laugh even as it makes her friends and family cringe. Especially when they find *and read* her secret notebook. Boy, is she in trouble then!

Follow her exciting, extraordinary adventures in these three breezy books, by Louise Fitzhugh.

☐ HARRIET THE SPY   43447-5-47 $2.95
☐ THE LONG SECRET   44977-4-92   2.95
☐ SPORT   48221-6-48   2.50

YEARLING BOOKS

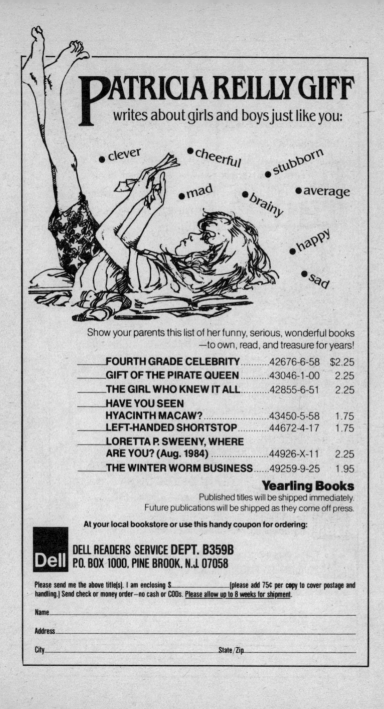